FROM USA Today BESTSELLING AUTHOR

ERIN BEDFORD

ALSO BY ERIN BEDFORD

The Underground Series

Chasing Rabbits
Chasing Cats
Chasing Princes
Chasing Shadows
Chasing Hearts
The Crimes of Alice
Hatter's Heart
Cheshire's Smile

The Mary Wiles Chronicles

Marked by Hell
Bound by Hell
Deceived by Hell
Tempted by Hell

Starcrossed Dragons

Riding Lightning
Grinding Frost
Swallowing Fire
Pounding Earth

The Crimson Fold

Until Midnight
Until Dawn
Until Sunset

Curse of the Fairy Tales

Rapunzel Untamed
Rapunzel Unveiled
Rapunzel Unchained

<u>Her Angels</u>
Heaven's Embrace
Heaven's A Beach
Heaven's Most Wanted

<u>House of Durand</u>
Indebted to the Vampires
Wanted by the Vampires
Protected by the Vampires
Embrace of the Vampires
Tempted by the Butler
Loved by the Vampires
Huntress of the Vampires

<u>Academy of Witches</u>
Witching On A Star
As You Witch
Witch You Were Here
Just Witch It
Summer Witchin'

<u>Children of the Fallen</u>
Death In Her Eyes
Fire In Her Blood

<u>House of Van Helsing</u>
Her Cross To Bear

<u>Fairy Tale Bad Boys</u>
Beauty and the Hunter
Wendy's Pirate

The Beast of the Fae Court
Granting Her Wish
Vampire CEO

FROM USA TODAY BESTSELLING AUTHOR

ERIN BEDFORD

HUNTRESS OF THE Vampires

HOUSE OF DURAND
BOOK SEVEN

CHAPTER 1
Piper

SWEAT DRIPPED DOWN MY brow. I swiped a hand over my face and ducked just as a blast of air slid over my head. I barely missed getting kicked in the face by a grinning Mizuki.

Mizuki's long black hair was swept up into a tight ponytail, the tail of it long and brushing the bottom of her backside. She moved as gracefully as a ballerina in her all-leather outfit that looked more appropriate in an S&M dungeon than in a training room.

Smirking at me, Mizuki twisted the handle of the practice sword in her hand, so it was pointed downward in some kind of samurai pose. Hell, most of the hunters here were trained in several types of martial arts on top of weapons training. Why the hell I thought Billy could make me one of them, I'd never know.

"Come on, vamp bait," Mizuki sneered, her olive complexion not even breaking a sweat. unlike me, who was about to pass out from overheating. "I thought you were superhuman fast. So far, you've only gotten knocked on your ass how many times now?"

I opened my mouth to answer.

"Six."

I snapped my mouth closed and glared at the man on the sidelines. "Thanks, Bishop, but when I want your help, I'll ask for it." He started to respond, but I cut him off with a hand up. "I never want your help."

"Never say never." Mizuki purred, crossing one leg over the other like a cat as she stalked me. "You never know, one of these nights, you might have Bishop at your back, and you will pray for his help."

"That's a scary thought," I muttered, shifting around the training room, so Mizuki didn't end up behind me.

Bishop snickered, crossing his muscular arms over the tank top stretched over his chest. He had one of those military cuts where his blonde hair didn't touch his collar or ears, but he kept it a bit longer on the top. If he hadn't been such an asshole, Bishop could be called attractive by some. Unfortunately, while I had the extra abilities as a human servant to Antoine, I couldn't go arm in arm with the guy and win. Bishop wasn't even one of the most prominent vampire hunters in the Atlanta Headquarters. Still, he had quite a bit of muscle on him. I trusted him to kill the vampires but not to keep me alive. There were several other vampire hunters I trusted over Bishop any day. Even Mizuki would do in a pinch.

Sure, Mizuki was supposed to train me to be a badass vampire hunter like herself, but she made no illusions that she liked me or the task she'd been assigned. I had a feeling she thought her skills were better used elsewhere. Couldn't say that I blamed her.

"Are we going to just dance around the mat all day, or are we going to train?" I tightened my grip on my own sword and held it up by my ear. I didn't have any fancy martial arts training over the basics that

Billy had taught me. I'd basically been hoping my supernatural speed and strength would get me through most situations. Mizuki had already taught me how wrong I'd been.

Mizuki's red-painted lips curled up slightly, and then she came at me. Taunting Mizuki was a little like poking a snake. You knew it was a bad idea, and yet you did it anyway. It was only a matter of time before she lashed out at you, but I wanted it to be on my terms, not on hers.

This time when Mizuki came for me, I ducked low, sweeping my leg behind hers. Mizuki fell to the ground, using momentum to roll before doing one of those impressive backbend jumps to land back on her feet. Even I was in awe.

"Neat." I quipped. Mizuki didn't respond. She came at me fast and hard, swinging her wooden sword at a rapid pace. Each hit I blocked sent a shock wave up my arm. I couldn't take much more of the pressure before Mizuki was going to break through my guard.

Not wanting to give her a chance, I pushed back from her, giving myself some distance. I did a fancy spin thing that I'd seen on television once, not really expecting to land a hit but wanting to confuse her enough to get a hit in.

Mizuki whacked me on the shoulder with her practice sword as I came back around. I grabbed her sword with my free hand and jerked her close. She glared at me behind eyes so dark and full of anger, it would make any vampire quake in place. Mizuki's other hand reached out to stop my sword from hitting her, but I had something else in mind.

Quickly before she could realize what I intended to do, I angled my head back and slammed it against the front of her nose. A crunching sound followed. Mizuki instantly released me, stumbling back to grip her nose, now dripping with blood.

I tensed for retribution. It never came.

Mizuki spit off to the side, leaving a blob of blood on the training mat and grinned victoriously. "Good. Again."

I limped into the Durand manor several hours later. My whole body felt like one big bruise. My bruises had bruises, and I had to do it all over again tomorrow.

Thankfully, it was still light outside, so the Durand family would be in bed. Or they should be. Antoine might be upstairs in his office working, but the others wouldn't come out of the basement until after dusk.

I tilted my head to the side, wincing—even that hurt.

Listening for either Gretchen or Darren moving around the house, I sighed happily when there was nothing. Hopefully, that meant I had enough time to get something to eat and then take a shower before I had to explain myself to my newest beau, Darren.

I loved the guy, but he could worry with the best of them. Even Gretchen didn't give me as much of a hard time as Darren did.

Each step through the foyer, through the dining room, and into the kitchen felt like I was getting hit with Mizuki's sword all over again. I'd hate to be put up against her with a real weapon.

Opening the refrigerator, I pushed aside the silver metal containers labeled with the guy's names on it. Drake had accidentally drunk Rayne's once, and it had taken a week to keep him from jumping the bigger vampire. In the case of vampire strength, bigger did not mean stronger.

My hand wrapped around one of my sports drinks, enjoying the cold bottle against my palm. I contemplated drinking the drink here in the kitchen but had a feeling I wouldn't be so lucky to be left alone that long.

Groaning, I made my way to the backstairs used for the servants of the household. While I technically wasn't a servant anymore - I couldn't very well be a maid and a vampire hunter at the same time, there just wasn't enough time in the day - it just didn't make sense to go all the way around to the main staircase.

Each step up the stairs made my bones burn as if they were on fire. Feeling absolutely terrible for myself, I used the railing to drag my body up each and every agonizing step. When I reached the top, I hung my head and whined. Taking a deep breath, I worked the last few steps down the hallway and into my bedroom.

Most nights, Darren and I slept together in his room. It was the bigger of the two and more comfortable to maneuver around. When I was spending time with the others, we rotated between my space and theirs, depending on what was going on.

Today, I was happy to be on my own. I loved the guys with all my heart, even Marcus, in some way. Though, we hadn't quite figured out if we are anything or not. Did one kiss make a relationship? Okay, it was more of a make-out session in a life or death situation, but taking blood was about like sex for vampires too. Did Marcus think we were more now?

I shook my head and cried a bit at the movement. I didn't have time to worry about my relationship status. If I didn't get in some cold water soon, my body was going to hate me even more than it already did.

Setting my drink on the nearby dresser, I didn't bother pulling clothes out yet and painstakingly pulled my sweat-soaked shirt over my head. My yoga pants were a bit harder to get off. They clung to me like a second skin, and each yank down my legs made a small whimper escape. I got one side off and tried to hop on one foot to get the other one off. Which only resulted in me ending up on the floor. Graceful, I was not.

I jerked the yoga pants the rest of the way down my leg and scrawled across the floor. Trying to stand was going to be too painful, and I just wasn't up to it. What happened to the super healing powers that came with this gig? I mean, I could hear far more than I wanted to, and God knew my nose had found new smells than I ever had the right to know. I was supposed to be harder to kill. So, why did I feel like I'd been run over by a Mack truck?

Flipping on the cold water, I hissed as I pulled myself over the edge of the tub. I flicked the switch for the showerhead and sat on the bottom of the tub while the cold water rushed over me. I tried to close the curtain, but even that seemed to be more than I was up for.

Once my muscles had relaxed enough for me to move without dying, I inched to my feet and closed the plastic curtain. Turning the shower knob, I changed the water over to a more moderate temperature. I leaned forward against the shower wall, placing my forehead against the cold tile as the water rushed over my aching body.

I didn't know how long I stood in the shower before the bedroom door opened. Not turning around, I listened to the soft footsteps cross the bedroom, and the clack of dress shoes hit the tiled bathroom floor.

"When did you get home?" Darren's soft voice asked from the other side of the curtain.

I cleared my throat, and even that made me wince. "Just a few minutes ago."

There was some shuffling, and then the curtain opened. Cold air brushed against my back and legs. Darren's naked body stepped up behind mine, his gloveless fingers trailing over my back. I tried not to flinch at his touch.

"They worked you hard today." No questions. No accusations. Just statements.

Not looking a gift horse in the mouth, I swallowed and breathed out, "Yeah."

"Have you seen any of the masters yet?" Darren pushed my hair over my shoulder, and his lips skimmed my skin.

"No," I shuddered, my body warming at just the feel of him near me. Even though I was so tired, I still reacted to him quickly.

"Antoine is in his office. Perhaps a visit is in need?" He made it a question, giving me a choice. Not demanding I go to our master. Though, calling Antoine my master was about as true as calling the mayor the master of every person in the city.

Laughable.

"Maybe later," I shifted around until I faced him, the water spilling over both of us. I leaned forward and pressed my lips to his, sinking into the feel of his body against mine. It wasn't just lust I felt for Darren. It was safety. Comfort. Friendship. Being one of the only other humans in a household of vampires will bring you closer than anything else. And I didn't see myself shacking up with

Gretchen. Though, her cooking was worth going lesbian for.

"You're hurting," Darren murmured against my lips but he didn't pull away.

"Am I?" I leaned into him, scrapping my nipples against his chest. "I had forgotten."

Smiling, Darren shifted away from me and picked up the nearby loofah. "Let me get your back."

My face might have felt like a big swollen muscle, but I found myself grinning as I turned around. "Yes, sir."

CHAPTER 2
Darren

"THIS ONE NEEDS YOUR signature. And this one. Initial here." I pointed at the line on the document before Antoine. "And that should be all for now." I picked the stack of papers off the table, tapping the ends to line them up.

I turned away from the desk, the next task already on my mind. Antione's voice stopped me.

"Yes, master?" I pivoted on my heel, waiting expectantly.

Antoine had braided his hair today, the long tail of it brushing the middle of his chest. He placed his fingers together in a steeple in front of him. His suit jacket had been discarded, and the top two buttons of his dress shirt were undone, exposing the pale skin beneath. If there was ever a poster boy for vampires, it would be Antoine.

"How are things?" his voice, which usually held a commanding no-nonsense sort of tone even when not using his powers, held no inflection at all.

I frowned slightly. My brows drew down in confusion. "I'm not sure what you mean, master?"

Arching a brow, Antoine angled his head to one side. "I refer to your wellbeing since coming back from our little adventure."

The temptation to snort at his wording was strong. I held back. "If one could call it such. I'm well. Happy to be home once more." Curious that he couldn't tell how I felt through our blood bond, I didn't point it out to him.

"And Piper?"

Ah. Things become clearer.

"We are...adjusting." I let the papers relax in my hands. "It's still a bit..."

"Too good to be true?" Antione finished for me with a small smile.

I inclined my head. "Precisely. Though, I do wish things had turned out differently." Piper had practically given up her freedom to save the Durands, binding herself to the vicious vampire hunter guild and their untrustworthy president, Vincent. In my opinion, not that anyone would ask for it, we should have saved Marcus and killed our way out. Giving the hunters an inch was only asking for an arrow in the back.

"I understand your hesitance," Antoine continued, shifting in his chair to fold one leg over the other. "None of us could have predicted our dear Piper would trade everything for us. It certainly has put us in a peculiar situation."

The way he said it made me pause. "What has happened?"

Antione sighed and picked up the silver letter opener on his desk, twirling it in between his fingers. He was fidgeting. Antoine never fidgeted.

"Antoine," I prodded further, dropping all formalities. "What is it?"

Curling his fingers around the handle of the letter opener, he stabbed it into the surface of his desk. "Certain acquaintances of ours have found out about Piper's new...position. I do not know how they have come by this knowledge, but they are determined to use it to their advantage."

I didn't like the sound of that. "The information certainly wasn't leaked from one in our household. Who is this acquaintance?"

Antoine leveled a look at me. "Morpheus."

My jaw tightened at the name. The owner of Club Dead, a notorious vampire hang out, had unfortunately helped the Durands find out where the vampire hunters' headquarters were. Morpheus was one of the less trusting of the master vampires. He wasn't as bad as Valentine, but only by a little bit.

"What does he want?" My words came out harder than I meant for them to be.

Antoine's expression went neutral. "What else? Guarantees that we won't sic our personal vampire hunter on him. Immunity from all crimes against him. Anything that the vampire council wouldn't approve of, naturally."

This time I did snort. "And he believes his favor was worth this?"

Smirking, Antoine shook his head. "Of course not. And yet it is in Morpheus's nature to push the bounds of honor."

"What are we going to do?" Suspicion leaked into my voice. I was having a harder time keeping control of my emotions when it came to Piper. I used to be able to take all these vampire politics in stride. Now I have found I lost the taste for them. Or perhaps I was just getting too old for it all.

"Do not look at me with such contempt." Antoine narrowed his icy blue gaze on me. "I do not plan to give Morpheus anything more than vague answers. I certainly will not promise him things I cannot do. Besides," his lips ticked up slightly, "trying to promise Piper won't cut off his head with her new group of friends wouldn't be truthful now, would it?"

I smiled in return. "She is quite a wild card." I frowned, thinking of the bruises and cuts that marred her body in the shower.

"You're worried. Why?"

He read me so easily now it was almost scary. Even after decades together, it was hard to get used to.

"I believe Piper would benefit from a visit and perhaps a bit of blood exchange." I tried my best not to break the promise I'd given

Piper. The one that kept me from telling the Durands all about the injuries she sustained while keeping us all safe. She didn't want to worry them for one, and the other, she didn't want them rushing in and doing something stupid.

So, I did what I could.

Antoine stared at me as if expecting me to give him more, but when I didn't, he nodded. "Very well, I will make a point to visit her today."

"Thank you, master." I bowed at the waist and turned on my heel, heading for the door.

"Darren." Antoine's voice was low this time, and I almost missed it. I paused but didn't turn back around. "You'd tell me if they were harming her in some way, wouldn't you?"

I swallowed thickly and nodded without looking at him. "Yes, of course."

"Good. That is all."

I hurried out of the room, knowing when I'd been dismissed. I wasn't a hundred percent sure Antoine had believed me, but I did what I had to do. We always hurt the ones we loved, especially when the other one was more stubborn than a mule.

CHAPTER 3
Piper

"THIS IS REALLY GOOD, Gretchen. Can I keep you?" I asked the older woman through a mouthful of the most delicious pulled pork I'd ever tasted.

Gretchen chuckled and wiped her hands on her white apron. "I think you'd have a bit of a fight in that area." She winked at me.

I sighed, wincing as the movement caused me to bump my bruises hidden beneath my long sleeve shirt. My bruises were healing faster than a human, but I still felt like I'd been run under a rolling pin. They'd turned from an ugly purple to a sickly yellow, and that was just enough to have some nosy vampires asking unwanted questions. Hence the hiding under long sleeves when it was sweltering outside.

"I suppose I'll just have to live with the fringe benefits of having you through the Durands." I sank my teeth into the slightly crispy bun, the barbecue sauce oozing out the sides of it as I bit off a substantial chunk.

"Are you trying to steal my cook away again, Piper?" Antoine appeared in the doorway of the kitchen one hand on the button of his suit jacket. He unbuttoned it as he crossed the room, slipping in between the barstools to stand beside me.

I swallowed and grinned up at him. "Every chance I can."

Antoine stared at me for a moment and then reached out. Freezing in place, my eyes widened as his finger wiped a stray bit of sauce from my face. As if in a trance, my eyes followed that finger all the way to his mouth, where he slid it inside, impossibly slow.

Swallowing for an entirely different reason now, I used my napkin to clean my hands off and shot a discreet look to Gretchen. However, the woman had worked with the Durands long enough to know when to make herself scarce. While I'd been watching Antoine like some kind of holy being, she'd slipped out the door unnoticed.

"Is there a reason for that little display, or do you just like the attention?" Embarrassed by my staring, I turned to my only friend, sarcasm.

Leaning his elbow on the counter, Antoine shifted closer to me and murmured, "Always."

I snorted. "That's a non-answer if I'd ever heard one."

Pursing his lips in displeasure, Antoine picked up a strand of my hair that had fallen out of my ponytail. "Why is it that I am unable to use my usual tricks to get what I want?"

I shrugged a shoulder and turned back to my food. "I don't know. Just lucky, I guess."

Antoine's fingers trailed down the bare skin at the neckline of my shirt, causing me to shiver. "I affect you so easily, and yet I cannot bring you to heel."

I laughed so suddenly that I found myself choking. Coughing, I reached for my glass as Antoine patted me once hard on the back. I jerked forward, spilling my water all over the remnants of my meal and down the front of my shirt.

Jumping up, the cold liquid soaking through the thin material, I found myself pressed up against Antoine. More annoyed than aroused by the position, though that was in there too, I glared up at him. "Look what you made me do? I'm going to have to change all over again."

Antoine didn't seem to be listening, his eyes dipping down to the wet cloth clinging to my breasts. "My apologies. I had simply meant to help. Though, I see that you do not need it." His gaze lifted to my face, and for some reason, I blushed. "Do you have to work tonight?"

I nodded. "Yeah. The bitch from hell wants to take me out on a hunt., so I have to do pre-mission preparedness, whatever that means."

The vampire in front of me scowled. "Hunting. Haven't they humiliated you enough with their so-called training?"

My brows furrowed. "Why are you acting like this? It's like you're determined to pick a fight now." I pushed away from him and slipped out of the tight space between chairs. "Remember, I'm the one who signed up for this so your lily-white ass could stop running."

"And at what cost?" Antoine snapped, pivoting to match my stance. "When will it be enough? After five years, ten years? A hundred years of servitude just to keep our family safe?" He stalked after me, my feet fumbling back until my back hit the kitchen table. "Or will it only be enough once they have claimed your life, and then as you American's say it, all bets are off?"

"Is this what this is about?" I gaped at him, my emotions running high. "You're afraid I'm going to die?" I reached for him, but Antoine stepped back, his facial expression closing down. Scowling, I grabbed Antoine by the face and jerked him down to my level. "Stop that. You're the one who started this conversation. You don't get to shut down now."

Once Antoine was over his initial shock, he pressed his thin lips tightly together until they became nonexistent.

Pressing my forehead against his, I stared him hard in the eyes. "I'm not going to die. You pretty much made sure of that when I became your human servant."

"I know about your training sessions," Antoine shifted back from me, and I let him.

"You cannot tell me you will not get hurt when you are covered in bruises."

I gaped at him, wondering briefly how he knew. Then I realized how. "Darren. Of course, he told you."

Shaking his head, Antoine grabbed my side. I doubted Antoine had touched me that hard, but his hand had hit one of the many bruises covering my body still, making me gasp in pain.

"Darren did not need to tell me. Any of us would have noticed."

I frowned, holding my side. "I thought I covered them all."

Antoine traced a finger along the neckline of my shirt, pulling it down exactly where a bruise hid beneath. "The blood is closer to the surface now. It's not much of a distinction, and I wouldn't have been able to decipher the smell had I not been aware of them." His lip curled up on one side. "Besides, your movements gave you away."

I winced. "That bad, huh." I let out a long sigh. "I don't know how I'm going to handle another day of training, let alone hunting. I can't even eat without being in pain."

"That is where I come in." Antoine stared down at me purposefully.

My brow arched at his tone. Then my eyes widened, and I shook my head, waving my hands in front of me. "Oh, no. I can't take blood every time I get hurt. I like my dreams vampire-free thank you very much."

Antoine pursed his lips to one side and then said, "You are being ridiculous. Is dreaming of me so bad you would rather be in pain?"

I opened my mouth to say, "Yes, the fuck it was," then stopped. The worry clear on Antoine's face made me pause. Was the inconvenience really worth the pain? Yes. My life was surrounded and consumed by the Durands. Even my thoughts weren't safe with Rayne's abilities. The only part of me that they didn't take over completely was my dreams. The question was whether or not Antoine's sanity was worth my squeamishness? No. It wasn't.

Letting out a deep breath, I sagged in defeat. "Fine. But just this once."

"And you will take a vial of my blood with you -"

"Hell no." I jerked back from him, crossing my arms over my chest. "I won't be treated like an invalid."

"If you would let me finish," Antoine snarled, flashing his fangs.

My eyes narrowed. "Fine. What were you going to say?"

"You will take a vial of my blood -"

"Why your blood?" I interrupted again, causing Antoine to groan. "Sorry, sorry. Go on."

Antoine watched me closely for a moment before continuing, "For emergencies. I do not want you to be bleeding out on the sidewalk and those hunters leaving you to die. Before you argue," Antoine held his hand up, cutting me off. "I trust you to keep yourself safe. I do not trust them. Do this. For my peace of mind."

I thought about it for a moment and then nodded.

"Thank you," Antoine cupped the side of my face and pressed a chaste kiss to my lips. "I know how hard it was for you not to argue with me."

I grimaced. "I'm not that bad, am I?"

Antoine gave me a look that said, do you really have to ask. Then said out loud, "It is part of your charm, no doubt. However, the reasoning for you to take my blood with you is because I am your master-" I opened my mouth to tell him no the fuck he wasn't. Antoine placed a finger over my lips. "Whether you believe so or not is irrelevant.

You are bonded to me, and thus, that makes me your master for all metaphysical purposes."

"Fine." I jerked my head up and down.

"Since I am your master, my blood is more potent for healing serious injuries."

All the huffiness in my sails went out. I sagged. "I guess that makes sense." My phone dinged with a text message. I pulled it out and glanced down at it. "Ugh. They need me to come in now." Shoving my phone into my back pocket, I lifted my gaze to Antoine's pale one. "If we're going to do this, we need to do it quickly."

Antoine sighed. "I'd have preferred to exchange blood in a more...sensual setting, but as time is of the essence..." He unbuttoned the cuff of his sleeve and pulled it up, exposing his wrist.

I arched a brow, smirking. "What do you want me to do? Bite you? I kind of lack the necessary equipment-" Antoine cut his wrist with the nail on the opposite hand. "Okay," I drew out the word, the blood seeping out of the bite, not at all appealing. "I guess that solves it."

Holding his wrist out to me, Antoine flicked his head in my direction. "Come, it will close soon."

Wrinkling my nose, I took the offered wrist and leaned down toward it. I tried not to think about what I was doing while I wrapped my mouth around the bloody wound. My eyes squeezed shut while my jaw worked. A coppery sweetness filled my mouth, and suddenly all the unpleasantness of the act vanished. My hands tightened around Antoine's wrist, pulling him tighter to me as I swallowed quickly.

I could feel the muscles in my body relax and heal. The bruises no longer hurt, and I suddenly didn't want to head into work today. A low moan escaped my throat as I leaned my body closer to Antoine's. Rubbing myself against the side of Antoine's front, I was pleased to find that he wasn't exactly unaffected by my actions like I was.

"Piper," Antoine breathed against my head, his hand touching my hair. "You must stop."

My eyes flicked up as I sucked harder, the wound healing beneath my mouth. I whimpered as the liquid came slower, no matter how much I urged it out. When I couldn't get it to come out faster, I bared my teeth, preparing to bite down.

"Stop." The commanding power of Antoine's voice froze me in place, my mouth open wide. "Release me." My hands instantly let go of Antoine's arm and stood, frowning at my actions.

"Why did I do that?" I added on, "I mean, not the part where I stopped. I got that and sorry." I flushed, remembering how hungry I had become. "I mean, why couldn't I stop?" I licked my lips, tasting the remnants of Antoine's blood on my lips. My lower body jerked. Startled, I stumbled back from him, needing some space between us.

"Do not feel alarmed. It is simply a reaction to our bond." Antoine explained, way too calm about it all. "Your body wants to be closer to me. Exchanging blood and other..." he waved a hand in front of him, "...bodily fluids."

I frowned. "I didn't have this reaction before."

"You haven't taken my blood directly from the vein since the binding." Antoine continued stalking toward me. My feet skittered back until I bumped against the counter. "I'm sure if you asked Darren, he would be able to confirm what you are feeling right now."

I swallowed, my mouth dry. "How do you know what I'm feeling?"

With one hand on either side of me, blocking me in, Antoine leaned forward until his nose brushed along my jawline. "I can smell the sultry scent of your desire. The quick upbeat of your pulse. Your thighs pressing together, trying to quell the need my blood has inspired." His chest pressed against me as his mouth hovered over mine. "There is no shame to it."

"I never said I was ashamed." I lifted my face, our lips brushing.

"Good." Antoine closed those few millimeters. His mouth nipped and pulled on mine, tasting himself on my lips before delving into my mouth with his tongue.

Moaning against his mouth, I grabbed a handful of that gorgeous silver hair and pulled him closer, my back arching into him. Antoine cupped my butt, bringing our middles closer together. I rubbed against his hardness, wrapping a leg around his waist to get even closer.

My phone pinged.

Fuck.

"I have to go," I muttered against Antoine's mouth. "They're waiting on me."

"Make them wait." Antoine ground his length into the junction of my thighs, making me gasp and groan. "You worked for me first."

I smiled and kissed him once more before pulling away. "Technically, I'm not your maid anymore, so it doesn't matter. I have to go." I lowered my leg and pushed against him, shifting out from between the counter and his body.

"Just because you do not do the job anymore does not mean you are not still employed by this household." Antoine turned and watched me walk to the door.

Pausing, I turned back to him with narrowed eyes. "Watch it. The hunters pay me for my services as well. I don't need your money. Plus, I have what I got from the house in Seabrick in savings. I could drop all this and live quite comfortably on my own."

Antoine's lips curled on one side. "You would miss us."

"I probably would," I countered. "But thankfully, we don't have to test that now."

"True."

"Exactly. See you."

"Piper."

Shifting back to Antoine with a sigh, I asked, "What? I have to go."

Antoine tossed something through the air. My hand automatically reached out and grabbed it. Opening my palm, I found a small vial of blood. Glancing up at Antoine, I frowned. "Did you already have this ready?"

"Of course," Antoine stated matter of fact. "Be safe."

I closed my mouth, cutting off anything I was going to say. I nodded. "Thanks. I will."

CHAPTER 4
Rayne

PIPER WATCHED MY EVERY movement. Her eyes flicking to different parts of my body as if trying to decipher which part she'd like to take a bite out of first. Unfortunately, for me that wasn't the case.

Move damn it.

Piper's thoughts fluttered through my mind betraying her true motives. I didn't need mind reading powers to figure that out. No. Sadly, there was nothing sensual about her gaze. Everything she was looking for was a weakness, some tell that I'd attack.

Sighing, I did what she wanted me to do and launched at her. I threw myself across the training room that was usually reserved for the twins and their workout equipment. It'd been converted to now have ample space for Piper to train. The majority of the weight machines were pushed off to one side while the floor had been covered in an off blue foam mat. The twins hadn't been too happy about having less space to work out, but we all had to accept the changes going on around us.

Piper included.

I had a half second to think I might actually hit the love of my life when Piper shifted to one side at the last moment, her wooden sword hitting me in the side.

"Why am I helping you do this again?" I grimaced as I rubbed the affronting spot. "Can't you just practice with the other hunters?"

Relaxing her stance briefly, Piper scowled. "Because I need to train against a real vampire, not a vampire hunter. While they may have superhuman powers too, it's not the same." She blew a strand of blonde hair out of her face. "Besides, they beat the shit out of me every time just to spite me, not to train me." Fucking Mizuki and her cronies.

Nodding, I cracked my knuckles. "I'm sorry. I would take this burden off of you if I could."

Piper gave me a soft smile. "I know. But there's no use in wishing. It is what it is. Now come on. I want to get some more practice in before I get called in again."

Shifting a foot back into a fighting stance, I prepared to attack again. While Piper had a weapon, I only had my hands and fangs to keep me safe. "More realistic," Piper had said. Realistic my ass. I knew for a fact several vampires carried weapons on them at all times because of situations like these. If you let your guard down, that was exactly when the hunters would strike.

"No weapons," I called out, making Piper frown. "What are you going to do if you're attacked and your weapon gets tossed or broken?" I pointed out with all seriousness. "You need to be able to defend yourself not just with an advantage."

Piper smirked. "Alright." She threw the wood sword to the side and lifted her hands into a martial arts stance she had learned from her trainer Billy. "Show me what you've got."

We circled around each other for a moment, each of us searching for an opening. I didn't want to hurt Piper but if it was what it took to keep her safe, I'd do it. I'd do a lot of things to keep her safe. Even if it meant making her hate me for it later.

Not holding back, I feigned left before dropping down and kicking out, sweeping Piper's legs out from under her. Before she could regain her balance, I was on top of her, my fangs at her throat but not piercing. "I win," I breathed along her neck. Then I felt something on my back. Something sharp. I froze.

Piper grinned up at me, her hand holding a dagger I'd never seen her pull. "I think that means I win."

Smiling back at her, pride swelled in my chest. "That's my girl." I leaned forward and kissed her neck, my hands moving from the mat to her hips.

"Rayne," Piper giggled, arching up to push me off. "We're supposed to be training, not playing around."

I laid on the floor and watched her stand up. "Yeah well how about a break? We can get all hot and sweaty the fun way." I wagged my eyebrows at her.

Shaking her head with a laugh, Piper re-sheathed her dagger in the holder under her pant leg. She was wearing a sports bra and sweatpants so there weren't many places for her to hide a weapon. I'd have to remember that next time.

"How about we finish training and then I'll think about it." She arched a brow at me. No funny business.

Pushing up to my feet, I held my hands out, showing I had nothing up my sleeves. Which in my tank top and gym shorts I literally had no sleeves. "Alright but I'm warning you. I'm not holding back anymore."

Piper's lips ticked on one side. "Good."

About a half hour later, I was even breathing heavily, and I didn't need to breathe! Old habits and all that. Piper had sweat dripping down her face and neck, sliding along her skin and between her breasts. It was quite distracting. Plus, she kept thinking naughty stuff to throw me off.

I'm going to bite that bubble butt of yours the second I get those clothes off.

My attack faltered by just a fraction of a second. It was enough for Piper to get the upper hand. She grabbed my wrist and pinned me to the mirror wall, my arm twisted behind my back.

"Give up," Piper purred into my ear, pressing her front tightly against my back. I could feel every inch of her curves and it was damn distracting.

"Depends." I licked my lips, glancing over my shoulder. "Are you going to follow through on all those things you were using to mess me up?"

Piper chuckled, her breath against my ear. "I'm just using the tools I have. Like you said, I won't always have a weapon."

"Oh, I don't think you'll have that problem." With my free hand, I reached back and groped a handful of her ass. Piper laughed and shifted away. "However, you know me. You know my abilities. If it were some other vampire, you wouldn't know if they had telepathic abilities or nothing at all."

I felt Piper shrug. "I'll just have to find out all I can before going up against them. Now," she pulled on my arm a bit making me wince. "Do you admit defeat?"

I paused for a moment and then nodded, "Yes. You win."

With a squeal of victory, Piper released my arm and did a little happy dance. She looked ridiculous and absolutely adorable. Without warning, I grabbed her by the arm and pulled her toward me. Pushing her up against the mirrored wall, I boxed her in, shoving my hips and hardened erection between her thighs.

"What are you doing?" Piper gasped, her hands held firmly over her head by mine. "I won."

I grinned. "No, actually, I think I did." I thrust my hips against her slightly, rubbing myself along her center. "Now, I plan to take my prize."

Piper angled her head back, her mouth looking pouty and tantalizing. "Well, I suppose we can call it a draw this time."

"That's my girl." I lowered my head toward hers. "I knew you'd come around to my way of thinking."

"Shut up and kiss me already." Piper pushed against my arms and caught my mouth with hers, pulling my lower lip in between her teeth. Her legs lifted and wrapped around my waist, effectively pressing her hot center against my lower abdomen.

Releasing her hands, I used one hand to hold the back of her neck and the other to cup her breast over her sports bra. Our mouths fought each other the same way our bodies had just minutes ago except this time we weren't looking for a winner.

More, please. Piper's words cried out through my head.

I tried to push my hand beneath her sports bra but found it suctioned tightly to her from the sweat and elastic. Not asking permission, I jerked on the front of it causing the polyester fabric to rip and her glorious breasts to come tumbling out.

Piper jerked her mouth from mine. "Fucking a, Rayne." She glowered down at her chest. "I just bought that bra."

Ignoring her complaints, I lowered my head and lapped at her skin, licking the salty sweat from her breast until I came to her nipple. Encasing it with my mouth, Piper quit complaining and arched into me, her fingers threading through the shaggy length of my red hair. I sucked her breast into my mouth as far as my fangs allowed me to.

Piper shifted in my arms, jerking on my hair at the same time as she pressed closer to me. Stop. More. Now.

People think that hearing someone's thoughts would make it easy to please in the bedroom. It did. Sometimes. Other times, the other person's thoughts were so broken up and scattered there was no telling what they were thinking. I had to rely on body cues as well at thoughts to get it just right and even then, who knew. Women were tricky that way.

Releasing Piper's nipple with a wet popping sound, I switched to the other giving it the same amount of attention. Piper's hips rotated against mine, the scent of her arousal filling the training room. She bucked and ground against me, trying to find some kind of friction. Withdrawing from her breasts, I licked and kissed my way down her stomach until I reached the top of her sweatpants.

"Don't you dare." Piper warned before I could even think to rip them off.

Grinning up at her, I pulled her sweats over her hips and down her legs, leaving her in a pair of tiny white panties. I knelt in front of her, pulling one shoe and sock off and then the other, before removing her pants the rest of the way.

On my way back up her legs, I kissed and nipped at her skin causing her to gasp and squirm. I paid particular attention to the back of her knee which made her hips buck rapidly as she tugged on my hair.

Please, Rayne. No more teasing.

"As you wish," I murmured against her inner thigh. I trailed my lips along her smooth and creamy flesh until I came to the white cotton of her panties. They were damp from sweat and her arousal, causing the material to turn practically see through. Brushing my nose along the line of her lower lips, over the outside of the material, I breathed her in. When Piper's breath hitched, I flicked my tongue out making her jerk in place.

"Damn it, Rayne." Piper pushed at my head, shifting her hips this way and that. "Just do it already, fuck."

Peering up at her from between her legs, I met her desire filled gaze. I watched her as I slid her panties to one side, exposing her folds to me and gave her one long lick. Piper sucked in a breath and shuddered as she let it out. Picking one leg up, I threw it over my shoulder, opening her wider to my view. Catching her arousal on my tongue, I lapped at her until I found that bundle of nerves that made her jerk and twitch beneath my mouth.

Closing my lips around it, I sucked as much as I could into my mouth being careful of my fangs. Piper's legs spasmed and I was in danger of getting my hair ripped out of my head as she came. Gently releasing her, I lowered her leg. Her knees gave out under her but I wrapped an arm around her waist as I stood.

Piper giggled. "Oops."

Wiping my mouth off with the back of my hand, I grinned at her. "Not a problem. I'll be your strength." I pushed my gym shorts down enough to release myself from my pants and underwear. "Hold on tight to me."

Piper wrapped her legs around my waist, her arms going around my neck. "Wouldn't this be easier on the floor?" Her words were cut off as I slid my cock into her hot center.

"What was that?" I asked, then thrust into her once more, cutting her off again. "I can't hear you." My mouth stayed in a permanent grin while Piper tried to come up with something to say.

Fuck you, Rayne.

I leaned forward until my lips hit her ear. "You already are."

Glaring up at me, Piper's face contorted in pleasure as I drove us both into oblivion. I supposed I could muster the energy to train with her more often. We all had to sacrifice something for this family after all.

CHAPTER 5

Piper

"GOOD JOB, PIPER," MIZUKI jerked her head in my direction, wiping her blade off on a cloth she'd pulled from God knew where. Seriously, the woman wore a lot of leather. It couldn't be comfortable.

"Thanks." I turned my back on her so she wouldn't see me grimace.

We'd just disposed of a nest of newbie vamps in downtown Atlanta. The sun hadn't even come up yet, so we were able to get the jump on them. Five of us against a nest of vampires. Which equaled out to about three per hunter. If the others found that troubling, they hadn't protested, so I kept my mouth shut and tried not to die. Thankfully, the vampires hadn't come into their abilities yet and basically ran around like chickens with their heads cut off the moment we busted through the door of the hotel room they were crashing in.

Seriously. A hotel room. Did they really think that was safe? The maid could have come in at any time and pulled the curtains back, killing the lot of them instantly. Of course, that's pretty much what we'd done once the vampires got over the initial shock of us busting into their nest. It was pretty easy to take them out once they were all cowering away from the streams of sunlight. Almost too easy. I'd felt kind of bad for them to be honest. Unfortunately, the fact that they'd been picking off drunken college students and dumping them in broad daylight kind of put a damper on my pity.

One of them had realized that I wasn't like the others and tried to appeal to me. "Why are you helping them? You're someone's servant."

I'd shrugged and said, "It's either them or you. I choose you," before shooting an arrow through his heart. Thankfully, we didn't have to worry about the cleanup. They had a separate team for that.

"Not bad, liar." Tristan bumped my shoulder as he walked by. The massive hunter hadn't been talking to me since he found out that I lied to him about being an actual hunter. I think I hurt the big guy's feelings. Still, he was more on my side than the others were.

The hunters wouldn't flat out say it, but I didn't think any of them agreed with their president's decision to bring me into their little group. They not so subtly had let me know they thought I was an undead whore and deserved to die with the rest of them. Luckily for me, they respected their leader's decision and had worked with me. Now, as far as watching my back? We were still working on that.

I touched the side of my neck where one of the baby vamps had sunk his teeth into me. My fingers came back bloody. Fuck.

"Here." Mizuki tossed me a plastic package with a white bandage in it. "You'll want to clean that when you get home."

A hunter by the name of Axel snorted. "Why? It's just foreplay to her."

I narrowed my eyes on Axel, the spiky redhead, who'd been nothing but a dick to me. "Getting bitten during sex is different than one trying to rip my throat out." I carefully placed the adhesive patch on my neck.

Axel shrugged. "Same difference to me. If you let those creatures bite you, then you're just as bad. You should have flaunted your neck more at them, making it even easier for us to kill them all."

Not willing to put up with it anymore, I stepped up to the taller hunter. "What did you say to me?"

His hazel eyes peered down at me as he smirked. "You heard me. You're not good for anything other than vampire bait. None of us want you here, so why don't you just go back to your master like a good like bit-" My fist swung out and pelted him across the face, effectively shutting him up.

"What was that, asshole?" I snapped, prepared for him to hit me back.

Axel didn't hit me. He simply spit blood out of his mouth off to the side and grinned. "Bitch."

This time I didn't hold back, I slammed my knee up and into his stomach, before bringing my elbow down on his back at full force. Axel fell to the ground with a groan. Sadly, still conscious.

"Hey, she can't do that." Bishop spoke up, taking a step toward us.

Mizuki stopped him with an arm.

"But she-" Bishop protested, but Mizuki shot him a death glare.

"Axel started it," Mizuki explained, sheathing her sword. When it seemed that Axel wasn't going to say anything else, Mizuki walked over to us. "Normally, fighting a fellow hunter is punishable by a week of extra duty, but seeing as he had it coming, I'll let it slide. This time." She squatted by Axel and flicked his forehead. "Next time you start a fight, you better finish it, or I will finish you."

Axel grunted in response.

Standing, Mizuki gave me one last passing glance before turning her back on me. "Get some rest. We'll be heading out tomorrow for another hunt."

I groaned. "Another one? Don't you guys ever take a break?"

It was Bishop who answered. "A true hunter never rests. They are always ready for the hunt. It's what we were made for. It's who we are." His expression firmly said, and I was not one of them.

Ignoring his provoking words, I waved a hand over my shoulder and headed for the gates of the headquarters where my ride was waiting. Typically I'd have driven my car, but Antoine was feeling a bit nervous about leaving me alone lately. The other Durands, unfortunately, had agreed. So, we compromised. Instead of one of them coming to pick me up every day, I had a car service come pick me up every day. The driver changed every time, and they couldn't be bought off even to stop at McDonald's. They had strict instructions to take me home, and that's it.

Sometimes I wanted to shove one of the hunter's arrows up the Durands' collective asses. I loved them, but they were so anal about some things. My safety for one. Not like that wasn't high up on my priority list either, but still, I'm able to handle myself. I didn't need them to handhold me—for example, Axel's bleeding form.

"Miss Durand," the driver inclined his head, his eyes only briefly flicking to the bandage on my neck, and the blood splatter on my clothing.

I gave him a tight smile. "Action movie. It's going to be awesome."

Relief filled the driver's face as he opened the door for me.

I didn't know if he actually believed me, but the excuse had worked well with all the rest of them, so I kept to it. What did I care what they thought? They were paid to get me safely home, not ask questions. I slumped in the backseat of the car and then sat back up when it caused my neck to ache.

The car began to move, and my mind wondered. How much longer would I have to do this? Was Antoine right? Would I be doing this until I either died or one of the other hunters take over for President Vincent and get rid of me? Sadly, I didn't see any other options. I didn't want to go back into hiding any more than the guys, and I couldn't do this forever. There had to be a way out of it. Or at least some vacation time, 'cause at this rate, they were going to run me into an early grave.

Wincing as I found a new bruise on my side, I fingered the vial of Antoine's blood safely tucked into a leather-covered pocket attached at my belt. I'd almost worn it around my neck but figured that would be too easily broken. Antoine had assured me the glass was made of stronger stuff than that but still better safe than sorry. So, I kept it in the special pocket, and no one was the wiser. Besides, I wasn't sure what the hunters would do if they knew I had it as a failsafe.

We finally arrived home before I passed out in the car from exhaustion. The driver pulled into the circular driveway and parked the car. I was up and out before he could open the door for me and headed for the door.

My feet dragged as I made my way up the walkway, my body aching in all-new fun places. Before I reached the front door, a figure appeared out from behind one of the stone columns. I immediately went into defensive mode, pulling my dagger out and pointing it in their direction.

Jack Biggs, attorney at law and my ex-employer from Seabrick, stood in front of me. His dark hair was mused, and a faint line of hair lined his jaw as if he hadn't had time to shave. His brown eyes were wide as he held his hands in front of him. Jack wore a suit with no jacket, his tie was loose around his neck, and his sleeves rolled up to the elbow. If he was here on official business, he'd have worn the jacket and not looked so comfortable. He and Antoine were alike in that manner. Except Antione was never comfortable.

"Holy shit," Jack cried out, backing up from me. "What the hell Piper?"

"Oh, sorry." I put the dagger away in the wrist sheath. My eyebrows furrowing, I returned my attention back to Jack. "What are you doing here?"

Jack's gaze was wary as he took in my form, and no doubt, the blood on my skin and clothes. "Bethany and I were worried about you. You quit so suddenly with no notice." Jack explained, though I hinted a lie in there, I doubted Bethany cared enough to question my sudden departure. "I went to your house, but you'd already sold it."

"I told you, I had a family emergency and had to come back home." I didn't offer to let him in the house. It was almost dark, and the guys would be up and about around now. "You didn't need to come."

Jack shrugged. "You weren't answering my calls. I needed...I mean, we needed to be sure you were okay."

I swung a hand in front of me. "Well, I am. I'm sorry you wasted your time. You can go home now." I moved for the door, and Jack grabbed my arm.

"Now, hold on a second. You appear in our lives as if out of thin air, and then suddenly, you have a boyfriend we never heard of, and then you mysteriously get sick. Then the next thing we know, you come back to resign without notice. Just some paltry excuse of a family emergency." Jack shook his head, his gaze hard. "I can't accept that. I'm a lawyer. I know someone trying to cover up something when I see it."

There was movement in the house. Shit.

I pushed Jack's hand away from my arm. If Jack was surprised by my strength, then he didn't show it. He did stand his ground, though. "Look, Jack. I can understand your concern, but my life is a bit more complicated than I led on. Frankly, it's none of your business. I haven't done anything wrong. So, unless you have something else to say, you can just leave."

Jack opened his mouth, no doubt to spout some more nonsense when the door opened behind me. The lawyer's mouth dropped open even further, his eyes widening as they lifted up and over my head. Meaning it could only be three of the people who lived in the house behind me.

Marcus was out on an errand for Antoine and wouldn't be back until this weekend.

Allister has made himself scarce lately. Who knew what he was up to? So, it only left one other beast of a man who could cause that kind of reaction in someone as confident as Jack Biggs.

Drake.

CHAPTER 6
Drake

"WELL, WHAT DO WE have here? Mr. Jack Biggs." I clucked my tongue and leaned my forearm against the door frame as I leered down at the little human. "What do we owe the pleasure of such a visit?"

The last time I'd seen the lawyer was back in Seabrick, flowers in one hand and soup in the other, coming to call on his attractive secretary while she was sick. Piper hadn't told us what really happened between the two of them, and Darren, when pressed, said it wasn't his story to tell. It pissed Rayne off of course, the hothead, but I'd let it go. After all, Piper was here with us, not him.

Now though, there was a problem.

"Mr. Biggs was just leaving." Piper turned slightly in my direction, placing a hand on my chest. I wasn't sure if it was to stop me from coming out of the house more or to shut me up. Neither was going to happen. "Why don't you get Darren for me. I'm going to need help cleaning this film make up off." She gestured at her form with a look in her eyes, saying, 'don't blow this.'

If Jack Biggs had half the nose I had, he'd know that wasn't fake blood coating Piper's skin. I'd know the coppery scent of blood anywhere, even vampire blood. She'd had a hard night. I probably should leave it alone...except I wouldn't. That's not who I am.

"Ah, Piper. The man drove for God knows how long to see you. Are you really going to turn him away at the door?" I kept my gaze on Jack, trying to keep my tone jovial, but even I couldn't keep the possessiveness out of my voice.

Piper glanced back at Jack, who had a hint of fear in him but actually swallowed it down enough when her gaze met his.

"It is getting late, and I did travel a long way." Jack took a step forward as if to appeal to her. "I didn't book a hotel. If I could just freshen up, eat, and maybe stay the night?" He angled his head, smiling in that good ol'boy way.

At first, I thought Piper was going to put him in his place. Tell him in no circumstances was he going to stay here, but then she stopped, and a broad grin spread across her face. A grin that said I was thinking wicked things, and none of them were going to happen to you. That face always ended up with one of us being kicked out of her bed, and I had a feeling it was going to be me this time.

"You're right, Jack. I'm sorry." Piper stepped closer to him and took his arm. "I apologize for my abruptness. It's been a long day. Why don't you come on in?"

Jack Biggs' smile grew until dimples appeared on either side of his face as Piper led him through the doorway, forcing me to either move or get run over. I moved, but not without giving the two of them a suspicious glare.

Behind Jack's back, Piper flipped me off.

I chuckled and shook my head, closing the door behind me. Well, this just got more interesting. I couldn't wait to see how the others reacted to Piper's guest.

Sticking my hands in the pockets of my gym shorts, I whistled a little tune, following after them. Piper led Jack through the dining room and into the kitchen, careful to avoid the basement door. Can't spook the puny lawyer, now could we?

The others were still downstairs, except for Antoine, who was up in his office as usual. I thought really hard at Rayne. Get your asses up here now. This was just too good to let it go unwitnessed.

I waited by the kitchen doorway, waiting for the others while Piper had Jack sit at the kitchen table.

"Darren, you remember my boss, Jack, right?" Piper forced a tight smile at the butler as she stepped away from him and walked over to the fridge. "Do you want anything to drink? Water? Tea?"

"Water is fine," Jack answered, his eyes staying on Darren, who stood by the stove working on dinner. Gretchen had the evening off thankfully, or she'd give me an earful about messing with Piper's friend.

I held back a snort.

If Jack was her friend, I'd eat my shorts. The man clearly wanted to fuck Piper and came all the way from Seabrick to do it. One would think after seeing Rayne, my brother, and me at Piper's house that he'd know well enough to stay away but apparently he didn't.

"I do remember," Darren finally responded, nodding his head in Jack's direction. "Nice to see you."

Jack's smile tightened. "Yes, you as well." Piper brought the glass of water over to Jack. "Thank you."

Piper nodded and turned her back to him, hiding her wince of pain.

I gave her a concerned look, but she discreetly waved me off and slid into the chair opposite of Jack. Looking over at Darren, he simply shrugged.

From the kitchen doorway, I heard movement downstairs and then a thunder of footsteps on the stairs. Piper paused in what she was about to say, tilting her head to one side and then narrowed her eyes in my direction.

"Am I missing something here?" Jack cast a look between us. "Should I leave?"

"No," Piper said at the same time as Darren said, "Yes."

Jack frowned harder and moved to stand. "If I'm too big of an inconvenience, I can get a hotel."

Piper waved him back in his seat. "You're fine. I promise."

Whatever Jack was going to say next was lost in Rayne's appearance in the doorway. "What's going on? I was just about to kick your brother's ass in -" his words trailed off as he finally took in the kitchen and our guest. "What's he doing here?"

I choked a laugh at the utter hostility in Rayne's voice. He never had been the one for subtle.

Piper shot Rayne a warning look before putting on a polite face. "Rayne, you remember my boss, Jack Biggs, from Seabrick? I believe you two have met."

Jack stood and offered Rayne his hand. "I'm sorry to appear so abruptly, but I didn't have a number to call. Piper's line was disconnected." He shot a questioning look in Piper's direction.

Piper gave a nervous chuckle. "Yeah, well, the cell phone service here is better than what I was using in Seabrick. I meant to give it to Bethany."

If that wasn't a clear indication of who she valued more in seeing again, I didn't know what was. It seemed that Jack Biggs didn't get the hint or didn't care. One made him oblivious, the other, stupid.

"So, you're doing films now?" Jack asked, taking a sip from his water.

Stupid. I'm counting on stupid.

Rayne snorted beside me, obviously listening to my thoughts. Piper shot us another warning look before answering Jack. "Uh, yeah. On the side, for a friend of mine. It's nothing big. Just a low budget indie film." She chugged water from her own glass as she tried to cover her ass. She was going a pretty good job of it until Marcus opened the backdoor and walked in.

Jack choked on his water, staring up at the large man.

Marcus was only a few inches taller than me and my twin Allister, but what he made up in height we made up for in style. Allister and I could charm the pants off of any woman or man. While Marcus had to get past the whole, 'I look like I eat baby giants for breakfast' reflex. Jack was right to be wary of him. Of all of us, he'd be the one to blow the whole thing.

"Why do I smell blood?" Marcus scanned the room with his dark eyes before landing on Piper. He didn't even give Jack a passing glance.

Crossing the room, he knelt by Piper's side and tilted her face toward him, searching her face and body for the extent of her injuries. Jack had barely gotten his breathing back under control, not that any of us had helped him.

"I'm fine, Marcus," Piper muttered, covering his hand with hers as she tried to soothe him. "Really."

"I thought you were making a film. Why would you have real blood on you?"

Marcus's head slowly shifted from Piper to Jack as if seeing him for the first time. Jack's face paled, and he gripped his glass with both hands, the fight or flight instinct clearly having been triggered.

Piper squeezed Marcus's hand in warning. "Marcus, this is Jack Biggs, the attorney I worked for back in Seabrick." To Jack, she said, "I am, and sometimes accidents happen, and you get hurt while doing stunts." She said it so forcefully that Marcus finally turned his gaze back to her.

Jack, having recovered from his initial fear, asked, "And you could smell the blood from the door? That must be one super nose you have there." He chuckled, trying to make a joke of it.

Marcus's face began to turn back to Jack, but Piper caught him, grabbing his nose playfully between her two fingers. "Marcus has an extra special nose. A regular hound dog. Aren't you?" She teased him with her voice and actions, but her eyes screamed, 'Don't fuck this up!'

Gently, far more gently than I'd ever seen the older vampire do, Marcus withdrew his face from her grasp and stood. "I will be in my room." He turned to leave but then paused and did something I'd never seen him do. Marcus bent down and kissed Piper on top of the head, smoothing his hand down the back of her hair before striding out of the room.

Piper sat with a faint blush creeping up her cheeks. She hid it with her glass, using the drink as a way to bide time. Silence fell over the kitchen. The only sound, the beat of the three humans' hearts and Darren puttering around the kitchen. To the outside looker, it would seem Darren was going about his business and not bothered by Jack's presence. Someone who has lived with the man for several decades could see the tension in his shoulders, the way he slammed things down a little more forcefully than usual.

I gave a sidelong look to Rayne, who shrugged.

"Dinner is almost ready," Darren broke the silence finally. "Will I be serving our guest in the dining room or the kitchen?"

Piper's head jerked toward Darren and then to us. This time it was my turn to shrug. It wasn't my call. He wasn't my guest. For all I cared, he could starve.

I must not have hidden my thoughts well because Rayne nudged me with his elbow. Forcing a polite expression on my face, I offered, "Wouldn't it be better to eat in the dining room where there is room for everyone? I'm sure Antoine and Wynn would love to meet your old boss."

There was a hint of malice in my voice that was lost on Jack, who grinned and stood. "Sounds great. Lead the way."

Rayne and I opened a space for Jack to pass through, barely big enough for him to pass by without touching us. Jack grinned nervously up at us and said, "Excuse me."

While Jack might have his head shoved up his ass, my intentions were not lost on Piper. She followed after her boss, her eyes narrowed on me and her teeth clenched. She stopped before Rayne and me, pointing a finger in the space between us. "I know what you're trying to do, and you better knock it the fuck off."

Rayne had the decency to look contrite.

I gave her an innocent smile. "Whatever do you mean?"

Piper's eyes narrowed even further before she pushed passed us and into the dining room. I exchanged a look with Darren who shook his head in disapproval but didn't wipe the smug grin off his face. At least, in this area, all of us were in agreement.

Jack Biggs had to go.

CHAPTER 7
Piper

I LED JACK TO a place at the long dining table, one near the end and as far away from where Antoine and Wynn sat as possible. I didn't know how they were going to react, but if it was anything like the others so far, then it wasn't going to be good. Even Darren had expressed his displeasure without saying a word.

"Just have a seat here," I told him with a pleasant expression. "I need to go change and wash up. I'm sure the guys will keep you company, won't you?" I forced a smile on my face that wasn't at all happy.

"Sure," Drake cheered, pulling up a seat at the table next to Jack. "Rayne and I will be happy to keep Mr. Biggs company, won't we, Rayne?"

Rayne sat at the end of the table and the opposite side of Jack, a vicious grin on his lips. "Oh, yes. We want to hear all about the man our Piper worked for."

"Your Piper?" Jack's brows rose and then looked at me in question.

I pulled at my braided hair and hurried to say, "I'll try not to be too long." When Jack wasn't looking, I flicked Rayne on the back of the head, earning me a scowl. I returned his with one of my own and thought at him. *Be nice.*

Rayne rolled his eyes.

Huffing, I shook my head and stalked back into the kitchen, where Darren was pulling a dish out of the oven. "God hates me, doesn't he?" I said in a low voice, leaning my upper body against the island, so I practically laid on top of it. "What have I done to be punished so? Is it all the sex? Cause I could cut down, you know..." I trailed off with a pout and then sighed. "Who am I kidding? That's not going to happen. I'm so screwed."

Darren placed the dish on top of the stove and removed his oven mitts. Walking over to me, he rubbed his gloved hand up and down my back. Darren had, unfortunately, started wearing them again when we came back from hiding. Though he only wore them while working. After hours, all his bare fingers and the rest of him was for me.

"You are not being punished. I do not think God cares how much sex you are having as long as you're a good person."

I stared up at Darren in disbelief. "Do you really think we have any say in the matter? For all, we know we've already sold our souls to hell by being bonded to a vampire."

In a flat voice, Darren responded, "If we're already going to hell, what does it matter?"

Jerking back up, I nodded and then winced. "You're right. No use worrying about it now."

"Are you really okay?" Darren brushed a strand of my hair behind my ear, cupping my face with his hand. "You have quite a bit of blood on you."

I smiled at him, covering his hand with mine and leaning into his touch. "I'm good. Most of it's not mine. Promise."

"Alright." Darren leaned forward and gave me a chaste kiss. "Then go clean up before our guest starts getting suspicious."

I glanced back at the dining room door. "You think? I'm just waiting for one of the guys to slip up and flash their fangs at him." I sighed heavily. Loud, rambunctious laughter came from the dining room, making me nervous. "I better hurry. Keep an eye on him? I don't want to have to hide a body today."

Darren smiled slightly. "Yes. Go on."

Casting one more worried look in the direction of the dining room, I headed for the servant stairs. Each step up the stairs reminded me of every punch and kick that had landed today. Even hunting during the day, vampires were still ten times stronger than me and they hit like it too. The trick was not to get hit. A lesson I was learning the hard way.

When I arrived in my room, I closed the door and sagged against it. For a moment, I didn't have to worry about anything. Not about the hunters. Not the vampires that I'd have to hunt and kill in the future. Not even the lawyer downstairs. For just a moment, I was only Piper. Ex-maid and lover to one human servant and five vampires, soon to be six if the way things with Marcus and I were going continued.

My face flushed once more in memory of how he had reacted to me in the kitchen. I unhooked the knife sheaths from my wrists and found the ones on my legs. I sat them on the nearby table and worked on undoing the leather belt of my pants. While most of the hunters used swords or poison-soaked arrows to kill their vamps, there were a few who used guns. A wooden tipped bullet would go through a vampire's heart just as well as a wooden stake. Though, you needed to blow their head off just to be sure.

As I unlaced my boots, I wondered briefly why I hadn't broken down from all the blood and gore I'd seen in the last week or so. My life was so much different than it had been when I began this job. Not only because of the men in my life, but the job I was doing now. I'd never been the squeamish type, but I expected to at least feel something about killing people.

Maybe it was because I was thinking about it now and not focusing on my own pain, but the moment my feet both were on the ground again, they were rushing to the bathroom. I fell before the toilet and vomited. I emptied everything out of my stomach, and dry heaved until snot and tears trailed down my face, and my hands were shaky on the sides of the toilet seat.

Something cold touched the back of my neck, making me jerk away from it.

Wynn stood over me, his hand holding a wet cloth to my neck. "Hello, love." He used his other hand to pull my hair away from my face.

"Hi." I smiled weakly, shifting away from the toilet and taking the cloth from him. "Thanks."

Wynn flushed the toilet and turned on the shower for me before kneeling. "Of course." He didn't ask me why I was throwing up. He didn't try to reason it. He simply knelt before me, pulling one sock off and then the other. When he reached for the bottom of my tank top, I leaned forward so he could lift it up and over my head. I sank back against the outside of the tub, flinching at the cold surface, but I didn't move away from it. I needed that difference in temperature right now.

Getting my pants off was a bit trickier with me sitting on the ground, I lifted my hips as Wynn dragged them down my legs with my panties. One would think it would be a sexy action, but the only thing I was thinking about was not passing out. I couldn't leave Jack down there with the wolves about to descend.

After we got my bra off, Wynn lifted me up in his arms and pulled the shower curtain back. I placed a hand on his chest, stopping him. "You're going to get your clothes wet."

Lips ticking up at the edges, Wynn answered, "I have more clothes. I only have one of you."

My chest swelled with what I hoped was love and not more vomit while Wynn stepped into the shower.

The water was cool. Cooler than I usually showered in, but given the circumstances, I didn't complain. Wynn sat me on the ground of the tub and turned to pull his shirt off but left his jeans on, his feet already bare. Kneeling in the tub, Wynn reached for my loofah and the soap. I tried to tell him I could do it myself, but he shook his head, this black hair clinging to his face and neck. "After all you've done for us, let me do this for you."

I didn't argue after that.

Wynn stroked the loofah across my skin, cleaning the dirt and blood off my flesh, being careful of my cuts and bruises. With most of the blood gone now, it was easier to see how hurt I actually was. It wasn't pretty. I was going to have to wear a long-sleeved turtleneck if I didn't want Jack to ask questions.

"I thought you weren't that hurt?" Wynn asked, smoothing the loofah down my back and across my stomach.

I leaned back in his embrace and sighed. "When your adrenaline is pumping, I guess you don't notice it as much." I let out a shuddering breath as the loofah brushed across my nipple. It pebbled beneath the rough material, and I expected Wynn to move on. Still, he left it there, moving in circles until lower things tightened and throbbed.

"What are you doing?" I breathed, leaning my head back to see his face.

"Taking some of the pain away," Wynn murmured, pressing his lips to my forehead. "Just relax."

The loofah switched breasts, each circle of it sending jolts of pleasure through my body and settling in my core. My thighs opened on their own accord, and Wynn took advantage of it. He pressed his knees up between mine, exposing me further.

"Wynn," I gasped, the showerhead positioned in just the right place to tease at my hot and slicken folds, but not enough to give my body what it wanted. Wynn's free hand brushed along my legs, not going close to my aching center. His power swept through me, making each nerve of my body more sensitive, and the teasing of the shower felt like a hundred tiny hands stroking along my skin.

I grabbed at the vampire behind me, looking for something to hold on to, my hips bucking up in response to all the stimulation I was receiving. I gasped and cried out for more, the pain in my body a faint memory.

Wynn held me around the waist, the loofah already forgotten. He brought me screaming my orgasm with barely a touch of his powers and the shower. When his fingers slipped between my thighs and delved into my folds, I scratched at his arm, at my arms, trying to find something to help relieve the building up inside of me. Two fingers pressed into me, moving over and over that one spot until my toes curled, and all I could see were spots before me.

When I could finally breathe again, I sagged in Wynn's arms, my limbs and every inch of me feeling like it was lying on a cloud. "Wow, Doctor Wynn, I didn't know you made house calls."

Wynn chuckled, causing my body to bounce slightly against him. "No one has ever mistaken me for a doctor." There was something in his voice that made me turn in his arms, my fingers stroked along the black Latin surrounding this Durand sigil tattooed on his chest.

"You know, you never told me what you were...you know before you became a vampire." The water was getting colder now, but I couldn't bring myself to move. I needed to know.

"I never told you? Really? I would think that after all this time, I'd have brought it up at some point." Wynn's tone was lighthearted, but there was something in it. Something aside from pain. It made me regret asking.

"You don't have to tell me." I shifted to get out of the tub. "We probably shouldn't leave the guys alone downstairs."

"I heard your boss was here." Wynn followed me out of the bathtub, turning the water off.

I dried my body and laughed halfheartedly. "Yeah, who knows what Rayne and Drake will say to him left alone."

"Of course," Wynn agreed, taking me by the arm, turning me toward him. I peered up at him, my brows drawing together. "My father was a farmer and a bastard. I was nothing and no one. I spent my days feeding the hogs and anything else my father demanded of me, including being his whipping boy for killing my mother at childbirth."

I gaped at him, my chest aching as I reached for his face. "I'm sorry."

Wynn pressed his face into my hand and closed his eyes. "It has been centuries, and yet I can still feel the sting of his belt on my back." He sucked in a breath and then sighed. "When Boris found me, I was hiding out in the stable, so my father, who had been drinking too much again, couldn't find me."

"How old were you?" My voice was quiet for some reason. Like talking too loudly would make it even more painful and real.

"Sixteen."

I flinched. I tried not to, but I couldn't control my face or my reaction.

Wynn noticed and smiled, sadness in his eyes. "Do not feel bad for me. I thought I was being saved, and at the time for a while, he did save me."

"But you were only sixteen," I gaped at him. "How is that even legal?" I shook my head and added, "Never mind, different times. What was it, like the 1700s?"

"Close. The 1600s." Wynn squeezed my hand and drew me close. "And clear those dirty thoughts from your mind. This is obviously the body of a man, not a child."

I grinned and snuggled against him. "I noticed."

"Boris may have had young tastes but he was not cruel enough to change one of us before we've grown completely."

"From what I know of him, the fact that he had even one saving quality makes me kind of feel bad about killing him." I paused for a moment and then shook my head. "Okay, I'm over it."

Rayne knocked on my open bathroom door. "If you two are done hiding out in here, Antoine is downstairs and about five seconds away from eating your lawyer friend."

I winced. "Alright. We're coming." I peered up at Wynn. "I better go save Jack from the men in my life."

CHAPTER 8
Antoine

WHAT WAS THIS HUMAN doing in my house? Sitting at my table and eating my food. Breathing my air...well, if I needed to breathe.

Drake had informed me this man was Piper's boss from when she was masquerading as a receptionist. This handsome man with the dimple in his cheek and this too sure of himself air that made me want to sink my teeth into him.

The only thing that saved him from becoming dinner was the fact that with each member of my family that appeared at the dinner table, the more unsure of himself Jack Biggs became. Rayne was beside himself with glee, his lips twitching ever so slightly, no doubt reading the thoughts of our unwelcome guest.

"So, you are all related?" Jack asked, shifting in his seat before he forced himself to stop. I could see the internal struggle on his face. He was trying so hard to be confident and not let his discomfort show. Most humans would have made excuses to leave already. While some humans craved our presence, others knew what we were from just being near us. They knew the danger even though their rational minds told them they were being preposterous.

Jack Biggs was one of those people.

He must care for Piper a great deal.

This couldn't be.

"Yes," I answered, his eyes flicking from my brothers, all but Allister and Wynn were seated at the table. Allister had left the moment the sun went down and Wynn was still upstairs taking care of our Piper. They were almost finished now.

Jack's brows furrowed. The question he wanted to ask was there on his face, but he didn't seem to know if he should ask it or not.

Rayne saved him from his suffering. "We're adopted." Jack glanced at him, making Rayne grin. "You were wondering why we don't look related?"

"Yes," Jack inclined his head, looking perplexed. "Your parents must have had their hands full with a house full of boys."

Drake released a boisterous laugh. "You could say that."

"Something more to drink?" Darren appeared at Jack's side, a pitcher of iced tea in his hands.

To the out-looker, it would seem that Darren was playing the perfect host. Happy to serve. Happy to be there.

To someone who knew him, they would see the tension in his shoulders. The white-knuckled grip of his fingers on the handle of the glass, just a tight squeeze away from shattering. The tightness around his eyes while his lips curled up into a pleasant smile. All signs that Darren was seething inside. He didn't care for this Jack Biggs and more than me.

"Yes, please." Jack held his glass up to Darren, oblivious to how close he was to getting his head bashed in by our usually calm butler. "Not that I'm not enjoying your company, but where's Piper? I thought she only went to clean up?"

Drake angled his head to one side and grinned. "She's just about finished. Seconds from being done."

"Yeah, she'll be coming any second now," Rayne added on, chuckling with Drake. Even Marcus made an amused sound.

Jack grinned in return, looking between us. "Am I missing something?"

"So many things." I found myself smiling at the lawyer. This seemed to unsettle him, which only caused me to smile more. "Tell me, Mr. Biggs, what brings you all the way from Seabrick? Certainly not to only check on our Piper?" I emphasized the word our pointedly. Best to remind him who she belonged to.

"Is it so hard to believe that I wanted to check on an employee?" Jack locked his eyes with mine, never wavering. It was braver than I thought.

"If you care for all your employees with such devotion, they are lucky indeed to have you for an employer." I rubbed the wine glass in front of me between my fingers, though nothing was in it. Darren had set the table for human company. Normally, Piper and Darren would eat their meals in the kitchen together. Sometimes we would all sit together at the dining table, each of us either drinking from our metal blood containers or eating what had been made for the evening meal. While the food was lost on us nutritiously, the taste was still a pleasant experience. It helped us feel human again in some ways. In others, regurgitating the food in the bathroom later, not so much.

"I try," Jack answered, taking a bite of some kind of pasta Darren had prepared for the night. I knew for a fact that Darren had prepared tonight's meal, especially for Piper. A celebration of sorts for getting through her first week of hunter training. Tonight, since Darren hadn't prepared enough for everyone, he simply placed the settings but didn't fill our plates. The fact that the imbecile before us was eating it was just salt in the wound.

"You're not eating?" Jack asked, pausing in mid-bite.

"We have dinner plans a little later," I explained with a tight smile.

"Yeah," Drake chuckled. "Wouldn't want to ruin our appetite."

Rayne covered a laugh with a cough.

Nodding his head in understanding, Jack went back to his meal. After a moment, when we didn't fill the silence, he asked, "What kind of work do you all do?" Jack shot a curious and slightly suspicious look around the table.

"A bit of this and that," I answered vaguely.

This was not the thing to say to a lawyer, apparently. It only made his suspicion of us deepen.

"Stop messing with him, Antoine." Piper appeared in the doorway with Wynn at her side. Jack pushed from the table to stand. His eyes took note of the arm Wynn had sitting low on Piper's hip. Piper smiled at Jack as she walked up to the table. "Antoine does a lot of real estate investments. Mostly overseas. He's the reason Darren and I were in Seabrick in the first place."

Too much information. Piper was giving too much information to this too suspicious lawyer.

"Real estate, huh?" Jack turned his gaze back to me. "Sounds kind of boring." His gaze slid around the room. "Obviously pays well, though."

I shrugged nonchalantly. "This house has been in the family for centuries. I cannot claim it all to my success."

"And the rest of you?" Jack peered around the table. "Do you do real estate too?"

Drake grinned and laced his fingers as he made himself more comfortable in his chair. "Among other things."

Piper moved around the room, taking the empty seat on the other side of Jack. Wynn sat next to her. Only one chair remained unclaimed. Piper noticed immediately. "Where's Allister?"

Drake snorted. "Who knows? He was gone moments after we woke."

Frowning, Piper didn't question him further. We couldn't risk discussing too much family business in front of the stranger that was Jack Biggs.

"There's more of you?" Jack questioned, surprised.

"My twin, Allister," Drake explained but didn't give any more details than that.

"I'm surprised you could pull yourself away from this house, Piper." Jack turned to her with a sly grin. "That you would come slum it in Seabrick when you have all this waiting for you." He implied more than he was saying, and Piper knew it. She ducked her head, her cheeks turning a lovely shade of pink.

"I do what I'm told."

Marcus snorted.

Piper's head jerked in his direction, and she tossed a green bean at him. "Hey, I listen..." she shifted in her seat as all of us stared at her and then muttered, "when I want to."

Jack chuckled. "That sounds like the Piper, I know." He leaned into her, his hand reaching out to touch her hand.

Too familiar. This human shouldn't know her at all. I blamed myself for it: myself and the vampire hunters.

She laughed politely and shifted her hand out of his reach.

Good girl.

Piper shot me a look as if she could read my mind. She couldn't, of course, but still, she knew me too well.

I arched a brow at her.

"So, how long will we be graced with your presence?" I asked, gaining me a warning look from Piper.

"Only the night." Jack didn't notice the exchange and was back to being his handsome lawyer self. "I only came to make sure Piper was alright. I have to get back to the office before my clients start to throw a fit. I swear, it's almost like having children." He chuckled and gazed around the table as if we were supposed to understand. When no one laughed with him, Jack turned to Wynn. "None of you are married? No kids?"

Wynn rolled his head in a lazy sort of way toward Jack. "No. No wife. No kids."

"None of you?" Jack pointed around the table. No one answered him. "A house full of bachelors, huh?" He huffed a laugh, and it wasn't happy. "How do you handle all the testosterone?"

Piper shrugged, and that pretty blush on her face appeared once more. "I get by."

Jack did not like that reaction at all.

I wondered how many women had actually ever told this man, no? Piper was appealing. Attractive. A challenge. I could see why he wanted her. Except there were plenty of other women he could be obsessed with, why Piper? Had she done something to make him think she was interested?

I glanced between Piper and the lawyer, trying to decipher what it was. What was I missing?

"Why don't you show Jack to his room?" Rayne prompted Piper with a stern tone, his

91

eyes flickering over to me. "You're finished, aren't you, Jack?"

Jack, confused for a moment, stood with Piper. "Oh, yeah. Thank you." He couldn't seem to wait for the chance to be alone with Piper. Six sets of eyes followed the lawyer and the woman who had changed all our lives out of the dining room.

Piper gave a warning look over her shoulder when Jack wasn't looking. I saluted her with my empty glass.

"Well, that was...painful." Wynn lounged back in his chair, his dark hair curling over his shoulders, those blue eyes so much darker than my own rolled in my direction. "Why did you not just command him to leave?"

I smacked my lips together and turned my face from him. "And piss off Piper? No, thank you. I don't want to sleep with one eye open tonight."

Marcus laughed. "Nor do I."

"Yeah," Drake leaned forward in his seat. "I'll bear that arrogant prick's presence for her, but he makes one move." He slapped his hand on the top of the table, making it shake. "And he's dinner."

"Patience," Rayne smirked as if he had a secret. "We may have lawyer on the menu soon enough."

"Did you hear something?" Drake's eager eyes filled with hope. "Please tell me you found something in that picture-perfect head of his that we can use against him? A wife who mysteriously died? A load of criminally guilty clients? Embezzlement? Give me something!"

Rayne laughed ruefully. "Sorry. He's basically perfect. Gives to charity. No criminals. He rarely even sees the inside of a courtroom. Does a ton of pro-bono stuff. He even visits his grandmother every Sunday in the nursing home."

"Damn." Drake sighed and slouched in his chair. "I was getting thirsty."

"Well, feed outside of the house and leave Piper's guest alone," Rayne said, his gaze on the door they had left through.

I straightened in my seat. "Does he know something?"

Rayne shook his head, his red hair falling over his eyes. "No. Not yet. He's suspicious of us, clearly."

Drake huffed. "You'd think our last encounter would have scared him off."

"I don't think he believes we're all Piper's boyfriends." Rayne leaned back in his seat and threw his feet up on the corner of the table. "He's not worried because he thinks Darren is the only one he has to compete with. And maybe Wynn." His gaze shifted to the other vampire. "The only ones he's seen physically intimate with Piper."

Drake scoffed. "So what, we need to fuck her in front of him so he gets the picture?"

Rayne shrugged.

"I do not believe it will come to that Draconius." I tapped my nail on the top of the table and angled my head to the side, listening to the conversation just above our heads. "I believe our dear Piper will handle the situation as we speak."

CHAPTER 9
Piper

RELIEF FILLED ME THE further away from the dining room I got. Even though the guys could still hear us, they couldn't make their snide remarks and underlying threats that Jack didn't understand.

Jack, on the other hand, took the alone time with me as an encouragement to hit on me. I was regretting letting him stay here with us: me and my need to prove a point.

"This place is really amazing," Jack commented, stopping in the hallway to stare up at a painting of some lilies in the water. "Is that a Monet?" His eyes widened, and he looked to me expectantly.

"I don't know. They have tons of art here. I couldn't tell the difference between a Picasso or a Monet." I shrugged. Not unless you're a Qing Dynasty vase. I laughed softly.

"What is it?" Jack placed a hand on my lower back, smiling at me.

Shaking my head, I stepped away from his touch. "Nothing. Just remembering something. The guest room is upstairs." I pointed as I moved toward the stairs. "This way."

Jack followed closely behind me. Too close. I could feel his breath on my arm as we walked up the stairs, and I didn't have to turn to know he was staring at my ass. Should have chosen the pants instead of work out shorts.

"So, how long have you lived here?" Jack asked. His voice held a forced nonchalance. As if he were trying to make me believe he didn't care about my answer.

I hummed and thought about my answer. "Not as long as I wish. We keep getting called away." I was sad to admit I'd spent more time in Seabrick than I had at this house. It made the need to keep the guys safe even more prominent. I didn't want to have to leave any time soon.

"Oh," Jack murmured as we reached the top of the stairs. I began to turn to the left where the guest room was, better than taking the chance of putting him near the guys. I didn't trust them not to try something in the middle of the night.

Jack stopped me with a hand on my elbow.

I glanced down at his hand and then up at him. "Yes?"

Giving me a small charming smile, Jack shifted in place strangely uncomfortable for one of the first times I'd ever seen. "I don't know a good way to ask this without sounding like a jackass. So, I'm just going to go for it."

I frowned, my brows furrowing together. "What?"

"You said you were dating Darren, right?" Jack's expression was more serious than the question required, and I was beginning to think I knew where he was going with this.

"Yes," I answered firmly. "I'm still dating Darren."

He huffed a laugh. "That's what I thought." Jack shook his head. "I came by your house while you were sick and the redhead one and Drake? Said they were your boyfriends too. I knew they had to be yanking my chain."

I shifted my weight onto my back foot and crossed my arms over my chest. "Not that it's any of your business, but they are."

"What?" Jack's head jerked back. "They're what?"

"My boyfriends," I said it slowly so he could understand. "I'm dating all of them."

Jack's face was an array of emotions. Surprise. Disbelief. Curiosity. Then finally, it settled on anger. "You know if you aren't interested then you can just say so, you don't have to make up such outlandish lies. Seriously, I thought you were better than that."

I scowled. "I'm not lying. And I wouldn't need any boyfriends to tell you I'm not interested. I'm not. I don't know how clearer I have to make it for you. I've been polite. I've tried not to hurt your feelings or my job, but now I just don't think subtlety is working." I huffed and jerked at my ponytail. Poor Bethany. That girl was head over heels for this jerk, and he was here trying to get in my pants. "If you can't accept that, then I don't know if you should stay here."

Jack quickly back-peddled, his hands up in front of him. "No. I'm sorry. I've just never known someone who has actually dated multiple people like that, especially not in the same household. Isn't that kind of awkward?" He tried to make light of it, smiling at me.

"Not really, no." I turned on my heel and led him toward his room.

"I don't mean to push my luck further..." Jack began making me stop and sigh. "But if you're dating them all, where do you sleep? I mean, do they take turns coming to you? Or do you go to them?"

Spinning on my heel, my annoyance already at an all-time high, I told Jack with a completely straight face. "Neither. We all sleep together in a big ass puppy dog pile. Naked. Sometimes we have so much sex we get stuck together and have to pry ourselves apart in the morning. Satisfied?"

Jack stared at me as if he weren't sure if I were telling the truth or not.

Rolling my eyes, I marched over to the nearby door. "Here. This is your room." I pushed the door open and gestured inside. "My room is down the hall on the right if you need anything. Darren is next to you, and the guys are on the other end of the house. I'd stay clear of them. Now, if you don't have any other questions, I'd like to eat my dinner." I glowered at him, daring him to ask me another dumb ass question.

He stepped into the bedroom, scanning over it briefly before turning back to me. "No, I think I'll be alright. Thank you for your hospitality. I apologize for any inconvenience I'm causing."

I jerked my head once. "No problem. Night."

Not waiting for him to return the sentiment, I stalked back down the stairs and into the dining room. The others had cleared out except for Marcus. I could hear Darren banging around in the kitchen, no doubt still pissed off by Jack's presence. Of all the guys, he was the most jealous of outsiders.

"Where'd everyone go?" I asked, sliding into my seat. Darren had made my favorite chicken fettuccine tonight. I took a big bite. Hmm. Yum. Still good, even lukewarm. I'd have to make sure to thank him.

"Antoine had business to attend to, and the others went to hunt." Marcus sat at the table, his metal container holding their daily ration of blood in it between his hands.

I turned my attention in his direction. "You didn't want something...warmer?" I swallowed hard and flushed. Talking about feeding always made my body heat up lately. Darren had explained to me that by being a human servant, my body expected me to give blood often and made it so that I would find it a pleasant experience.

When I had to donate to Marcus, it was more than a pleasant experience. More like orgasmic. It had made things between us...complicated.

While I had told Jack I was dating them all, I didn't actually know that for sure. I mean, Marcus and I exchanged a couple of kisses and some blood, but we hadn't had sex. We hadn't even said much to each other since then. I honestly didn't know what to say or how to go about it. It made sense that I would end up with all of them. I'd already basically screwed my way through the family as it was. What was one more?

It wasn't like I didn't like Marcus either. He was sweet. He didn't talk much, but what he did say was always to make sure that I was alright. Before he'd been captured by the hunters, I'd thought Marcus only thought of me like part of the family, nothing sexual at all. However, our little feeding session had changed things between us.

Now, he asked after my wellbeing as usual, but he always found a way to touch me. Brushing my hair behind my ear, touching my arm, or even just kissing the top of my head. I thought it would make things uncomfortable. It didn't. I liked that he wanted to be near me and touch me. He was so big, and having him around made me feel safe and dainty. Not that I would admit I like feeling small around him. That was the last thing I needed right now.

Marcus spoke low, his dark gaze on the table before him. "I thought you might like company while you eat."

"Oh." My brows shot up. "That's so nice of you. But..." I skimmed around the table. "It's kind of silly for you to sit all the way over there." I offered him a small smile as he lifted his head up.

Those dark orbs locked with mine for a moment before he was suddenly not there anymore. I startled as he appeared in the chair at the end of the table, right next to me. I giggled lightly. "I don't think I'll ever get used to that. Even with my extra senses."

Marcus's lips twitched. "I am faster than most."

I pushed some noodles around my plate and studied him. Marcus usually had all the looks of a soldier to him. Short hair, clean-shaven, and muscles for days. Add on the fact that he kept his facial expression so guarded it was hard to tell what he was thinking unless he wanted you to know.

I shoved my fork into my mouth, thinking.

Each member of the house of Durand had an ability that came with being a vampire. Antoine could command anyone with his voice and sometimes even his very presence. He could even control crows and see through them as well. It was a nifty ability. If only he'd stop worrying so much. Those crows are hard to explain when I was out training or like today on a hunt.

Rayne's ability was the most annoying and yet most useful of the others. He could read minds. Anyone's. It made it hard to keep anything from him. Which also made it easier for the guys to stay safe from their enemies. Though, it did make it feel like you didn't have any privacy around him— somethings you just didn't want your boyfriend to know about.

The twins each had their own ability as well. Drake had that mesmerizing gaze you always heard about in the books and movies.

He has literally convinced me out of my pants without ever saying a word. It was an interesting experience for sure.

Allister didn't like to use his power. He'd only showed it to me once. Allister had a gifted tongue, that was for sure. Even more than just the normal ways. His voice could literally convince you to do anything he wanted you to do as long as you were in hearing distance. It was a bit different than Antoine's gift, where it was more of an automatic response. Allister's made you want to do it. Like it was your idea in the first place.

The most fun of the abilities had to be Wynn's. Just thinking about the things he could do with just his mind alone made my skin ache. There was a reason the others didn't want him to use his powers against me in the beginning. I could see myself killing just to be at the mercy of Wynn's powers. If you could orgasm with just a look, you would too.

Marcus, though...he was still a mystery to me.

"So, is that all you can do?" I prompted. "You're stronger and faster, right? Anything else?"

The vampire before me tilted his head slightly, confusion in his eyes. "Is that important to you? Our abilities?"

The way he said it made me frown. "No. Not really. I mean, they're nice to have. Definitely gives us the advantage, but it doesn't get my motor going if that's what you mean." I paused and blushed. "I mean, besides Wynn."

Marcus nodded in understanding. "My abilities are more defensive than offensive. I cannot make anyone do what I want with my voice or even my presence. I cannot give you pleasure as Wynn does or read your mind, like Rayne. I take on more of the reconnaissance work because it is harder for me to get caught." He stopped, and his face grew grim. "When I am caught, I can heal faster than the others as well as I have a higher resistance to the poisons the hunters use. Obviously," he huffed bitterly. "I cannot keep myself from starving."

I nodded in understanding. "Hey, those all sound like good things to me. I mean, not the starving part, but then we figured that out as well." I winked at him and grinned, wanting to see that rare smile on his face.

I wasn't disappointed.

"So, what should we do about Jack?" I enunciated his name with a scowl. "He's being more of a pain in the ass than I expected."

"I could always get rid of him."

I gave Marcus a look. "We aren't going to kill him. Though, if he keeps trying to hit on me, I may change that decision later."

Marcus's fingers tightened around his container. Reaching out, I placed my hand on one of his large ones and squeezed slightly. He looked up at me.

"I'm just kidding. I can handle Jack Biggs." I said with distaste and then smiled at Marcus.

Marcus stared back at me, his expression softening as he placed his other hand on top of mine. "Yes. You can."

The tension in the room thickened the longer he looked at me. I didn't want to look away, but I wasn't sure what to do next. Marcus was so different from the others. I basically just had to treat them like guys to figure them out. Well, except Antoine. He was just an ass who apparently got off on me telling him to fuck off. It made the sex all the better though.

Marcus thankfully took the lead, shifting in his seat so that he leaned across the table.

I angled my head up as he lowered his down to mine. My lashes lowered in anticipation of what was to come. Would it be like before? When we'd been in the dungeon of the vampire hunter's guild, we basically tried to devour each other with our kisses. However, we were both running high on adrenaline and the blood-feeding. I didn't know if that was an anomaly or if it was always that way with Marcus.

The first faint brush of Marcus's lips slid across my cheek. First one side and then the other, skipping over my lips each time. I found myself trying to turn my head toward him with each pass, getting more frustrated when I was left wanting.

My eyes flipped open only to find Marcus staring right at me. Those dark orbs, so brown that they were almost black, bored into me. I found myself staring back at him, unable to close my eyes or look away as he lowered his face once more.

His mouth captured mine, this time in a chaste but firm kiss. One that felt much different than the others with my eyes wide open. More intimate somehow. My tongue dipped out to taste him, but Marcus moved away.

"Have a good night, Piper." Marcus stood, his gaze on me until he left the room.

When he was out of my sight, I released a long breath and grabbed the side of my head, utterly turned on just from one little kiss. "Fuck."

CHAPTER 10

Darren

RUINED. EVERYTHING. ALL OF my carefully planned work, destroyed. And why? Because of that ridiculous self-absorbed, thinks he's better than everyone, Jack Biggs.

Why did he have to come here? Why now? We were doing fine without the added drama. Piper had begun her training. She was finally getting confident in herself and the path she had chosen. The others were not as accepting of it as she would like them to be, but they'd come around. What other choice did they have?

I tossed the pan with what was left of the fettuccine I had specially prepared for Piper and myself into the sink. It hit the steel basin with a loud twang, making me wince at the sound. Still, it felt better to cause some chaos instead of doing what I really wanted to do, which was punch that smiling lawyer in the face.

Glass shattered everywhere after I squeezed a cup a little too hard. "Damn." I stared down at the pieces that had lodged themselves into my hand and then down at the mess on the floor. Jaw tightening, I stalked over to the sink and was careful of the glass as I knelt on the ground. I used my good hand to open the cabinet beneath and searched for the first aid kit.

"Hey," a soft voice came from behind me.

I jerked, hitting my head on the top of the cabinet. "Arggh," I groaned, sitting on the ground and clutching my head with one hand, the other bloodied one out in front of me.

"Jesus Christ, Darren, what have you done to yourself." Piper tiptoed around the glass on the floor and crouched down beside me. She looked over my hand and then the mess on the floor. "Have a disagreement with the kitchenware?"

I pursed my lips and winced again. "Something like that."

"Here," Piper forced back a smile, reaching for my hand. "Let me."

I allowed her to take my hand and baby me for a moment. She pulled a large piece of glass from the side of my hand, and I sucked in a sharp breath.

"Some of these are too small for me to get," Piper murmured. The comment seemed more to herself than to me. "I need some tweezers."

"There's a first aid kit," I jerked my head toward the still open cabinet.

"Oh," Piper glanced away from my hand to grab the small white box.

I watched and wallowed in my pain while she set the box down and riffled through it. She'd changed out of her bloodied hunter clothes and into her usual pajamas, a pale pink tank top and plaid shorts to match. Unfortunately, today she had worn a bra, and I couldn't distract myself with the line of her nipple pressed against the thin material as she pulled the small shards of glass from my hand.

"I'm sorry about tonight," Piper said, not looking up from my hand.

I cocked my head to one side. "Why?"

Piper pulled her lower lip in between her teeth as she concentrated on a particularly stubborn piece. "Ah, ha! Got it." She lowered the tweezers and met my gaze. "About dinner. I forgot you had been planning on us having a romantic evening together."

"It's alright."

"No, it's not." Piper shook her head, returning to work on my hand. "I should have remembered and not let Drake get to me. He just pushes my buttons sometimes. Just such a smug asshole, and after the day I had, I just lost it. Next thing I know, I'm inviting my ex-boss, who I don't even like to stay at our house."

"Understandable. I, too, have felt the need to lose it when it comes to dealing with the twins." I gasped as she pulled the last piece from my hand.

"There. All done." Piper pulled a bit of bandage out to wrap my hand. "You should wash that first. Then bandage it. Wouldn't want to get an infection, now would we?"

I sniffed, holding back a laugh. "There is no worry for infection. One of the benefits of being a human servant is we are immune against all illnesses. No colds. No infections." I stood and went to the sink, turning the water on. I hissed as I put my hand under the running water.

"Well, that's just nifty." Piper stood and went to the pantry, returning with a broom and dustpan. "That would have been nice to know before. Anything else I should know?"

Rinsing the remaining blood from my hand, I took a clean dish towel and carefully dried it, wincing with each press of the towel. "Besides the things you already know about, not really." My brows furrowed as I tried to think about what else she might need to know that I hadn't told her.

Piper finished cleaning up the glass and replacing the broom and pan. She leaned on the counter next to me, taking the bandage she had sat out and began to wrap my hand. "That's good. I'd hate to have random ability pop up in the middle of a fight." She laughed slightly. "Most of the other hunters hate me as it is, I don't need another reason for it."

When she finished tying the bandage off, I placed my hand against her face, staring into her light brown eyes. "How are you doing? Really?"

Piper gave me a self-deprecating smile and shrugged. "I'm fine."

I stared at her a moment longer, trying to find some shadow in her gaze that said she was lying.

"Really, Darren." Piper leaned into my hand and turned her face, pressing her lips to my palm. "I'm fine. I'm...adjusting." She let out a long breath and turned out of my embrace. "It's just hard, you know. I have to be this whole other person now. I'm not just little Piper Billings with no future and no prospects for one. I'm Piper Durand, ex-maid, a vampire's human servant, and hunter now. It sounds like something out of a movie. Except the ending isn't a happily ever after."

I frowned. "Why do you say that?"

Piper arched a brow at me. "Come on, really? Do you really think this is going to end well for any of us?"

"I don't see why not." I didn't like where she was going with this. If Piper was having doubts, then she might let her guard down, and something might happen to her.

"There are only a few ways this can go," Piper huffed, crossing her arms over her chest. "Either I'll get killed on the job by another vampire. Or one of the hunters will kill me out of some self-righteous need. Or Vincent will get tired of me and kill me. Or I try to break away from them, and they kill all of you and de facto me. So, see? No one wins. I should just give up now. Save us all the heartache and stress of it."

"No, you shouldn't." I stepped in front of her and grabbed her hands in mine. "The Piper I know wouldn't give up. She wouldn't let all this fear and doubt fill her mind and heart."

"She wouldn't?" Piper leaned her head back to look up at me, her lips twitching with a smile.

"No, she wouldn't." I squeezed her hands.

"And why not?"

I slid my hands around her waist and drew her closer to me, her arms going around my back. "Remember when you told me about your plan?"

"Yeah. You thought I'd lost it." She laughed bitterly.

"But I gave in eventually. Do you know why?" I pressed my forehead against hers and stared into her eyes. Piper shook her head once. "Because you were so sure of yourself. So determined to save everyone, even if that meant dying yourself. And you did it. A little human girl turned vampire servant infiltrated the big bad vampire hunter's lair and not only saved one of our own but struck a deal with their leader to keep us all safe."

"But at what cost?" Piper murmured, her gaze dropping from mine. "The vampires I killed today. How do I know they were even bad? How do I know I'm not just doing Vincent's dirty work? They begged for their lives, Darren. And I didn't care. It was them or me."

I cupped her face with my hands and leaned back to meet her troubled gaze. "That's all it is for anyone. Chance. Survival. Maybe they are using you, but we're using them as well. To keep ourselves safe."

"Evil done for a good reason is still evil, Darren." Piper's eye watered, and she blinked them away. "I'm afraid of what I'm going to become if I keep this up. What if by the end there's nothing human left of me?"

"Then, I'll be here to remind you." I lowered my head until my lips brushed hers. "I'll remind you with every touch, every kiss, that you are human and alive. Not some killing machine."

Piper pressed up into my touch, holding me tightly in her arms. When she released me, she blinked up at me and asked, "Promise?"

My heart ached for all the pain and uncertainty I saw in her face. I never wanted this for her. I'd have fought harder to keep her out of it if I had thought she'd listen to me. Now, all I could do was this. I could promise this to her because that's all that I had to give her. If I could ease her suffering just a little, then I would do it ten times over.

"I promise."

CHAPTER 11
Piper

I was wrapped up in Darren's arms when my phone went off. I untangled myself from him and leaned over the bed, searching for my discarded phone. Grabbing it, I saw an unfamiliar number on the screen.

"Hello?" My voice was hoarse from sleep. I cleared it and tried again. "Who is this calling at..." I glanced at my phone again—"Freaking midnight. Someone better be dead or dying," I warned, already throwing my legs over the bed in preparation.

"Someone's about to be."

I frowned, my brows drawn together at the voice. "Mizuki?"

Instead of answering me, she said, "Meet me in Savannah. We just got word of a vampire club there."

"There is?" I pretended not to know what she was talking about. I couldn't bring up Club Dead on my own. I couldn't be that premeditated about it. The mattress moved behind me, and I knew Darren was awake. He placed his hand on my shoulder, and I waved him off. "Why are we going there?"

"Why else? To kill vampires." She hung up the phone, and I was left blinking down at a beeping phone.

"What did she say?" Darren asked.

I shook my head and stood. Turning the light on, I went to the closet. "She wants me to meet her in Savannah. At Club Dead."

"But that's Morpheus's club," Darren reminded me.

"I know that." I jerked on a pair of jeans and searched for my bra. "The jerk has it coming anyway. Now I have an excuse."

"You can't kill him."

I paused in the middle of putting on a long-sleeved black shirt. "Why not? He's a dick and an abuser." I jerked my shirt over my head. "After what he did to me and tried to do to Rayne, if any vampire deserves to die, it's him."

Darren walked across the room to me, still completely nude from our previous activities. For a moment, I was distracted by the expansion of his muscled chest, the line of his abs, and the hair that trailed down from his belly button to one of my favorite appendages.

I felt myself flush as I bit my lower lip.

"Stop looking at me that way, or you're going to be late." Darren's eyes darkened as he stopped a foot away from me. "And we owe Morpheus. We can't kill him until that debt has been paid."

My gaze jerked up from Darren's body, annoyance crossing my face. "I don't owe him anything. It wasn't me that needed his help. I figured out where the vampire hunters were without going to him."

Darren took me by the shoulders and smoothed his hands up and down them as if I were a startling calf. "Still, if you kill him or let him be killed without warning him, the other vampires will see it as a breach of conduct. Failing to uphold our side of a bargain is one of the vampire laws that the Council upholds above all else."

I snorted. "And killing one's maker? That's not against the law?" I paused and looked at him. "Council? What Council?"

Dropping his hands from my arms, Darren stepped back and went to the dresser. He pulled out a pair of pajama bottoms and slid them on. "The vampire Council resides in Italy where they can watch all their little peons as if they were the Pope." He made a disgusted face showing how highly he thought of that idea.

"Why am I just hearing about them now?" I watched him move around the room, getting dressed as I went about finding my weapons.

"The Council does not step in unless forced to. They do not want to get their lily-white hands dirty." Darren found a white t-shirt and covered his delectable body with it. Sad. "They didn't come after us for killing Boris because he was grotesque and made it harder for the vampires to stay under the radar. He needed to be put down. We just made it easier for them."

I remembered the blood-red of the Durand's maker, Boris, and shuddered. His teeth resembled that of a shark's mouth. His skin was loose and rough as if he had a skin condition though it was from living too long rather than any outside force. His ears were pointed and his nails were sharp enough to cut someone's throat. There was no way Boris could pass for human, and those who thought otherwise were just fooling themselves.

"So, what?" I slipped my dagger into my boot and fastened the other one into place on my wrist. "If we don't keep our promise, they're going to kill us?"

"Something like that." Darren crossed the room to stand beside me. "There is also the fact that they don't know you are working with the hunters. If they find out..." he sighed and shook his head. "Let's just say killing us will be the least of our worries."

I huffed. "Fine. I won't kill Morpheus." I moved away from him and stalked toward the door.

Darren called after me, "You can't let him be harmed by the hunters either."

Freezing in place, I twisted around to glare at him. "So what, I'm supposed to protect him now?"

"No." Darren shook his head. "But, I believe a call to forewarn him will do."

I swallowed and shook my head from side to side. "No. I can't do that. The hunters will know I tipped them off if the club is empty when we arrive."

Darren met me at the door. "Morpheus understands the rules. We have to warn him, but he cannot warn the others. He doesn't want to out you anymore than we do."

"Why?"

"And lose his advantage? He might need you again in the future. Morpheus knows what's at stake." Darren opened the door for me and gestured me out. "Go. I'll let Antoine know what is happening. We wouldn't want you to be late."

I followed him out into the hallway and down the carpet. I paused outside Jack's door. "Crap. What do we do about him?" I pointed at the closed door.

"Hopefully, you will return before we have to tell him anything." Darren placed a hand on my arm and kissed my cheek. "Be careful."

I frowned harder. I didn't like this. There were too many variables that could go wrong. Warning Morpheus seemed like a bad idea. I'd much rather have shoved a stake through his heart myself than let him getaway. Oh well, perhaps I would be able to do it another day.

With that happy thought in my head, I marched down the stairs and to the cars. It was too late to get the car service, and Antoine wouldn't be able to insist on it if I was already gone. I jumped into my little POS car and cranked the engine. It sputtered to life from disuse, and I smiled. It was nice to be back in something of my own.

I loved the Durands. They had given so much to me, but sometimes I missed my old life. It was certainly less exciting. Less life or death. Except it also didn't have them in it. I could admit that I would miss them if they were gone. I didn't know what I would do with myself if I lost them.

I sniffed and wiped at my eyes. No time to get emotional, I had a two-hour drive ahead of me.

Setting my phone's GPS to Club Dead, I cranked up the music and sang my heart out while I sped away from the house. Unfortunately, it only took about ten minutes before my phone was ringing with Antoine's number.

"Ugh," I groaned, clicking the button to answer the phone. My car didn't have any of that nifty built-in Bluetooth capabilities, so Antoine's voice came out crackling over the speakerphone.

"Where are you?"

I winced at the bite in his words. "I'm driving."

"Why did you leave without your driver?" There was arguing in the background, but I could only make out Rayne's voice.

"There wasn't time," I explained, keeping my eyes on the road. "Look, I really need to use my phone for directions. Last time I didn't exactly drive myself."

"Piper," Antoine growled my name through the phone. "This isn't the time to play the independence card. You will turn around and wait for us to decide the best course of action."

"I will do no such thing," I snapped in return. "Look, you want to be safe? This is the price you pay. I'm the one in harm's way instead of you. You can't keep me from doing my job."

"Yes, I can. I ca-"

I interrupted him before he could finish his sentence. "You what? You'll use your powers on me? Then what? We'll be right back to where we were a few weeks ago. Let me do this, Antoine. You just focus on making sure the Council you never told me about stays off my ass. Got it?"

"Piper, there are things we need to talk about."

"Sorry, can't hear you!" I raised my voice as if I was losing the signal. "I'm going...tunnel...call..." I hung up the phone and put it on Do Not Disturb mode.

Antoine would be pissed, of course. He was such a control freak he could hardly stand anyone telling him no, let alone the shit I made him put up with. I hadn't been lying, though. This was my fight, not his. He couldn't step in every time I did something he disagreed with. Vampire master or not, I had to do what I agreed to do. I'd keep them safe. No matter what.

When I finally arrived in front of Club Dead, I had more than a dozen missed calls and a massive amount of texts and phone messages. I ignored them all. Shoving my phone into my pocket for safekeeping, I climbed out of the car and grabbed my extra ammo from the passenger seat. I made sure my guns were secure, and the ammo was attached to the belt on my jeans before making my way over to Mizuki.

The neon light from Club Dead filled the sky, leaving bits of shadows in their wake. Ironically, it wasn't the vampires hiding in them but the vampire hunters. Mizuki stood with a dozen more hunters at her back, waiting for me.

"Isn't this a little overkill?" I asked, glancing at all the muscles she'd brought with her. Even Tristan had joined the fight, and he usually stayed away from me at all costs. Something about broken trust and all that. Couldn't say I blamed him.

"We're going into a club for vampires. Who knows how many are in there?" Bishop scowled, his arms flexing through his shirt angrily.

"Woah, hold your biceps." I held my hands up between us. "Have you even checked out the place yet? Had anyone go in?"

"No," Mizuki answered with a scowl. "Unfortunately, the proprietor of this place has kept the blueprints and other information out of public consumption."

"So, we're going in there blind?" I gaped at her and then shook my head. "How did you even find out about this place?"

"Why? So you can go tell your boyfriends?" Tristan hissed from beside Mizuki.

Mizuki held her hand up, quieting him. "How we get our information is none of your concern. Your job is to help us kill vampires."

"Bad vampires," I corrected her. "Yeah. None of the humans here have been forced to do anything they don't want to do. They want to be here."

"And how do you know that?" Tristan snarled at me. "I bet you and your boyfriends come here all the time. Just rip open a vein and go to town."

"You don't know what you're talking about," I bit out through clenched teeth.

"Enough, both of you." Mizuki looked between the two of us and flicked her long black braid over her shoulder. "You're right. We don't have any information about this place. That's why we need you."

I jerked my eyes away from Tristan and frowned at her. "Me? What am I supposed to do?"

"You're a human servant. Surely, you can enter here without there being any suspicion?" Mizuki questioned, arching a perfectly shaped brow. "Perhaps, even draw some of them out so we can even the odds."

I gaped at her and took a step back. "But you don't even know what vampires are in there. You can't just kill them all."

Mizuki's hand shot out and grabbed my wrist, keeping me from moving further away. "This is what we do, Piper. We hunt vampires. This place is full of them. There's no such thing as a good vampire. They're just showing you the best parts of themselves. Underneath all those pretty faces are monsters. All of them."

I ripped my arm from her grasp and glared at her. "I don't believe that." I tried to turn away and leave, but Mizuki's voice stopped me.

"Are you backing out on your part of the deal?"

"What?" I slowly turned back around. "What did you say to me?"

She kept those dark orbs on me, her gaze hardened and cold. "Just tell me now so I can let the President know that Durand is back on the menu." The hunters behind her tittered with unreleased hostility. "They want them, you know. Just because we stopped hunting them doesn't mean that our blood doesn't still sing to find them. All it would take is one word and -" She drew her finger across her throat, her lips curling into a smile.

I let out a hard laugh, staring at the lot of them. "You call yourself the good guys, but from where I'm standing, you're just as bad as those you hunt or worse. At least, they don't pretend they're something they're not."

"I need your answer, Piper. Are we hunting Durands tonight?" Mizuki provoked me, her tongue tracing her teeth as if she could taste them right now.

I pushed down all my anger and outrage and closed my eyes. When I opened them, I snapped, "Fine. Wait here."

"Wait, how do we know she's not going in there to warn them?" Bishop asked, his eyes locked on me.

Mizuki never looked away from me as she said, "She won't. Not if she wants to keep her precious Durands alive."

I shook my head in disbelief and turned away. How had I ended up in this mess? I should have just killed them all rather than striking a bargain with them. Now there was an idea. Realizing how bloodthirsty I sounded, I pushed the thought away and focused on what was in front of me.

Slipping out of my gun holster, I handed it to Mizuki.

"What are you doing?" She took the guns from me and held them as if they were babies.

"They'd never let me in the front door with all my weapons," I explained, removing the knives on my wrists. The one in my boot I kept because they couldn't see it, but all my visible weapons had to be gone. "I'll be wanting those back." Without another word, I walked away from them and into the nearby entrance of Club Dead.

The music pounded in my veins the same way it had the first time I'd been at the club. The long narrow hallway wasn't quite as ominous as it had been before. It gave me time to compose myself as I made my way into the club. I didn't know what I would do to fulfill Mizuki's request. It wasn't like I knew that many vampires. I couldn't just pick up a few and ask them to leave with me...could I?

In the central area of the club, the dance floor was packed to the brim. Vampires and their pets, dates, whatever they were calling their human companions, writhed against one another. Though most of the vampires kept their feeding to the booths and couch areas set up around the club, some didn't wait for privacy, sinking their fangs into their dates right there on the dance floor.

Thankfully, I didn't have to wait to find someone to trick into their untimely death. A pair of vampires, men, approached me just then.

The first one was taller than me by almost a foot, his eyes hungry as they swept over my form and settled on my neck. He was bald and had a crooked nose. I wondered if it had been broken when he was human. He flashed his fangs at me and reached a hand out to touch my face. I almost jerked away and then remembered why I was here.

"What's a pretty girl like you doing in a place like this?"

I offered him a flirty smile, lowering my lashes and then peering up at him from beneath them. "Just looking for someone to party with."

"We're great company." The second one had that flippy kind of hair you saw in teen heartthrob magazines, and he looked all of sixteen. I guess not everyone cared about making sure someone was full-grown before they were changed. "Why don't we find a seat and you can tell us all about you?"

I smiled up at them and said, "Actually, I was thinking we could go somewhere more private." I moved in closer and placed a hand on each of their arms. "I have a hotel room down the street."

Broken nose guy chuckled in the way men do when they know they're about to get laid while floppy haired guy pressed his face to the side of my neck and inhaled. I froze against him, not wanting to spook him.

"Oh, yeah, let's get out of here," floppy haired guy said, flashing me a fang toothed grin.

I linked my arms through both of theirs, scanning the room once more as I tried to get a decent headcount. We moved down the long hallway, the two vampires on my arms, whispering filthy things they were going to do to me once we were alone. Had it been my own vampires, I'd have probably enjoyed the dirty talk, but as it were...I happily threw them to the wolves, so to speak, once we were out the door.

"They're all yours," I quipped, darting back inside before the two of them realized what I had done. I played the game with a handful of other vampires delivering each and every one of them to the waiting hunters outside.

"How many more are there?" Mizuki asked, stopping me before I could go back inside.

I tallied them up in my head. "At least another dozen."

"What of the owner?"

I shook my head. "Haven't seen him."

"Him?" Mizuki arched a brow. "Do you know the vampire who owns this establishment?"

I quickly backtracked my words. "Uh, no. I don't know him, just of him."

"Then maybe you can play the game once more with him."

Arguing was not worth the waste of breath. I knew for a fact that Morpheus wouldn't be here. Antoine would have made sure to take care of that. Instead, I made my way back into the club and then to the bar. Might as well pretend to look for him and then head home when I fail.

On my way to the bar, a familiar laugh caught my ear. I spun on my heel, my heart beating like a drum in my chest. No. No. What were they doing here? They're going to get themselves killed. Why would they come here?

I pushed through the handful of people clustered around the couches. When I reached them, my worst fears were confirmed. Sitting on the couch with a woman beside him, fang marks on her neck, sat Allister Durand.

My fear was replaced with a wave of anger so palatable I could hardly speak. I forced myself to calm down and stalked over to the couch, rounding to the back of it where I could easily see the brunette woman leaning into Allister, the intent in her face clear to anyone who saw it. When Allister didn't discourage her, I couldn't hold back anymore.

I kicked the back of the couch, causing the whole thing to tumble over with Allister and the flirty blood whore. Allister, too shocked by my actions, didn't immediately understand what was going on until I had my knife out and at his throat. "What the hell do you think you are doing?"

CHAPTER 12
Allister

IT TOOK ME A moment to realize who the person was holding the sharp edge of a dagger to my neck. "Piper? What, what are you doing here?"

I winced as she pressed the dagger tighter against my throat. "I asked you first, you rat bastard."

We were gathering a crowd, and at the sake of not causing Piper to end up as dinner, I waved them off and tried to push up onto my elbows. Piper didn't give me an inch.

"I think it best if we take this elsewhere. Don't you?"

Piper noticed the crowd of hungry vampires and gritted her teeth, pulling away from me reluctantly. "You're right. This isn't the time or place." She grabbed me by the collar of my shirt and jerked me up with more strength than I expected.

"Allister," the woman, Yvaine, who had been my companion for the evening, reached for me, placing a hand on my arm. "Who is this woman?"

Before I could answer, Piper jerked me away from Yvaine and hissed, "Hands off. He's taken." A bit turned on by this new aggressive Piper, I allowed her to push me through the crowd and toward the back of the club.

"Not that I'm not enjoying your manhandling, but you never answered my question."

Piper shoved my shoulder. "You never answered mine."

Just then, before I could answer, the front door burst open, and hunters came pouring in.

"Shit. We don't have time." Piper dug into her pocket and pulled out her keys. Pushing them into my hands, she ushered me toward the back door. "Go. My car is out back."

I stared at her blankly.

"Go. You idiot. Before they see you."

"But what about you?" I couldn't just leave her behind. My brothers would never let me hear the end of it.

"I'll be fine. I have no doubt they will use your being here as an excuse to take you out." Piper shoved at me once more, and I had no choice but to do as she asked.

Hurrying out the back door, I kept to the shadows as I made my way to Piper's old vehicle, the one she had arrived in when she first came to our home. I was too big to sit in the front seat comfortably, so I squeezed into the back of the car and laid down, hiding from sight.

The shouting from inside of Club Dead could be heard through the door the hunters had busted down. I feared for Piper's safety, but as she had told me, she'd be fine. The hunters thought of her as one of them, and my being there would only put her in danger.

It felt like the fighting went on forever as I waited huddled in the car like a coward. I was tempted to phone Antoine and the others but didn't want to draw attention to myself. The car door opened all of a sudden, and I jerked up, flashing my fangs, and prepared to attack the person who had opened the door.

Piper gasped and then scowled. "Sit back and put those away before you get hurt."

I closed my mouth and relaxed back into the seat. "How'd it go?"

Piper cranked the car and peeled out of the parking lot without looking back. "How do you think it went?"

Leaning forward in between the front seats, I caught the metallic scent of blood filling my nose. "You're hurt." I placed my hand on her side, my fingers coming away wet.

She flinched away from me. "I'm fine. It's just a scratch."

"It doesn't smell like a scratch."

Letting out a long puff of breath, Piper murmured, "I'll be fine. Let's just get home."

"That's two hours away. You'll bleed out or wreck before then." I brought my wrist up to my mouth, sinking my fangs into my skin. Blood bubbled up from the wound as I offered it to her. "Take my blood. Heal yourself."

Piper sniffed and pushed my arm away. "I'd rather bleed to death."

"Well, I wouldn't. It would kill me if you died, let alone what Antoine would do to me if I let you die when I could have saved you." Piper leaned her head away from me, and I snarled in annoyance. I grabbed the back of her head and shoved my arm against her mouth. She struggled against me, the car jerking all over the road. Thankfully, the road was empty enough because of the time of night that we didn't hit anyone, but we were in danger of going off the street.

When I couldn't smell her blood as prominent as before, I released her. She shoved my arm away from her and swiped at her face.

"You asshole. Don't ever do that again."

"Yeah, yeah." I fell back against the backseat. "What were you doing at the club, Piper?"

Piper glared at me through the rear-view mirror. "My job. What's your excuse?"

I shifted uncomfortably in my seat. "I was feeding."

Her shoulders stiffened. "It looked like a hell of a lot more than that to me."

Grunting, I tried to figure out how to explain to her what happened that didn't make me look like an utter asshole. "It wasn't what it looked like."

"Really?" Piper asked incredulously. "Because you looked like you were getting real cozy with your dinner."

"So, what if I was?" I snapped in return, tired of the accusation in her voice. "It's not like you notice me that way."

Piper went quiet and then pulled the car over and shoved it in park, turning around in her seat to stare at me. "Is that what this was all about? You feel neglected?"

I pressed my mouth closed, my jaw tightening at her glare.

Biting out a laugh, Piper shook her head with a disbelieving smile. "I can't believe you. I'm sorry that between running for our lives and getting my ass handed to me, all to save your vampire ass, that I haven't spent as much time with you as you wanted." She looked down and then back up to me, the salty scent of her tears in the air. "You know of all of them, I would think you would understand."

"Why?" I asked, wanting to reach for her, to comfort her, but holding back. "Why would I understand? I'm always the other brother. One of the twins. Never just me. Just Allister. You only wanted me when you had both of us together. You haven't given me a second thought since then."

"Jesus fucking Christ, Allister!" Piper unbuckled and climbed over the seat into the back with me, sitting next to me on the driver's side. "You have the worst timing to be insecure."

I just shrugged. "Not like I planned it."

Piper dragged a hand over her face. "You know. We already have my ex-boss staying at the house, and the hunters are pushing our agreement to the limit. Not to mention Morpheus trying to call in his favor. I thought the one thing I wouldn't have to worry about was you all."

"Again, I say why?"

"Look at you." Piper gestured at me with a bitter laugh. "I mean, all of you have basically walked off the pages of Men's magazine. If anyone should be insecure, it should be me."

I reached out and pinched her chin between my fingers, turning her face to me. "I don't know what you mean by that."

Piper gave me a watery smile. "Look at me. I'm playing the big bad vampire hunter, but I'm just a girl. How am I supposed to keep you and the others happy for my lifetime, let alone forever?"

"Oh, Piper." I drew her into my arms and brushed my fingers through her hair.

"What if you all get tired of me? How do I get over that?" She muttered into my chest. "I'm bonded to Antoine, how do I get on with my life when I'll always want to be with him? With all of you?" Piper lifted her head from my chest and looked up at me. "How can you possibly love me forever? And what if you find someone else, like tonight? How do I deal with that?"

"Hey." I brushed away the tears that slid down her face, licking my thumb to taste the saltiness of it. "Hey, listen to me. Nothing happened with her. I promise. I came here to feed, and maybe I flirted a little bit more than I should have, but nothing ever came of it. I just wanted to feel wanted. I never imagined you were just as insecure about us as I am." I offered her a small smile.

"And now?"

I laughed. "Now, I feel like a first-class jackass and can't apologize enough."

Piper grabbed my face between her palms and pulled me down to her. Our mouths crushed against one another, nipping and pulling on my lips until a sharp sting of pain filled me. Then she did it all over again.

It was as if she were trying to punish me for daring to look elsewhere for attention. I wouldn't be making that mistake again.

Climbing into my lap, Piper shoved me back against the seat of her car. I chuckled at her aggression and then groaned as she rotated her hips against the front of my pants. Grabbing her ass, I pressed her down against me so she could feel how hard I was for her. Only her.

Piper pulled back from my mouth with a gasp of breath. "I'm not fucking you here in the car."

"What?" My disappointment evident in my voice.

She pushed away from me, smiling. "I mean it. This was just..."

"Just what?" I smoothed my hands up and down her back, arching up to kiss her again.

Dodging to the side, Piper slipped out of my lap and sighed. "I'm not having sex in the back of my car. God knows when it's been cleaned last. Plus," she pulled at her shirt and grimaced, "I'm gross and bloody. Not romantic at all."

I leaned my head back and took a calming breath. "Fine. Yes. You're right."

Piper smirked at me, pushing my shoulder. "Don't look so disappointed. If we get home before sunrise maybe, we can continue this at home?"

Grabbing her by the wrist, I pulled her closer to me, lowering my mouth to her pulse. "Very well. I suppose I can wait."

She gasped as I licked along her pulse. I laid a kiss on it and released her.

Taking her arm back, Piper stared at me for a moment longer before climbing back into the front seat. My eyes locked on her jean-clad ass, and I held back another groan, adjusting myself in my own pants.

When Piper dropped into her seat again, she paused and lowered the rear-view mirror to look at me. "Hey, Allister?"

"Yeah?"

"Are we good?"

I smiled. "Yeah. We're good."

CHAPTER 13
Piper

THE SUN HAD BARELY touched the horizon when I pulled the car into the garage. Thankfully, the closed garage was connected to the house and Allister was able to get inside without being torched.

We were laughing at the close call, our hands already finding ways to touch one another in the excitement of what was to come as we walked into the kitchen. Darren sat at the table with a cup of coffee and my weapons on the table in front of him. Mizuki sat across from him at the table, a cup in front of her as well, but it hadn't been touched.

I stepped away from Allister, a frown on my lips. "Mizuki, what are you doing here?"

Mizuki's gaze wasn't on me but Allister. "I was bringing your weapons back. You left in such a hurry, you forgot them."

"Oh." I moved forward to the table. "Thank you. You didn't have to come all the way out here. I could have gotten them from you later."

"Yes, but I wanted to see if what Tristan had seen was true for myself." She glanced between Allister and me. "And now, I have."

I kept myself between Allister and Mizuki as if I could hide him from her hateful gaze. "What are you talking about?"

Mizuki finally locked those dark penetrating eyes with mine. "Did you or did you not warn Morpheus of our coming?"

This, at least, I could answer truthfully. "No. Of course not."

"Then you admit you lied to me when you said you didn't know who the owner of Club Dead was?"

I paused and made sure to word it very carefully. "I have met Morpheus before. But I'd hardly say I know him. And nor are we on good terms. I want him dead as much as you do."

"Do you?" Mizuki arched a brow. "Because if you were willing to risk our operation to save your master," she gestured to Allister, "what is to say you didn't try to save others?"

Allister stepped around me, and I tried to stop him. "Don't."

He shrugged me off. "I can speak for myself."

"Then speak, vampire." Mizuki stood, using that towering figure of hers to her full advantage. Though, on someone like Allister, who was about the same height, it didn't have as much of an effect.

"Piper did not know I was there tonight, or I would have stayed home."

"Would you have?" Mizuki asked tauntingly. "Because my intel tells me you have been to the club every night since you came back from hiding. Or am I wrong?"

I looked to Allister, willing myself not to overreact. "Is this true?"

Allister turned his head toward me but didn't lose sight of the hunter before him. "I told you why."

"But you didn't tell me it was every night." I shook my head, wrapping my arms around myself. "How did I not know this? Did you know?" I shot a look at Darren, who only stared at Mizuki in response. "Was I the only one who didn't know?"

Mizuki sniffed a laugh. "What did you expect when you are dealing with monsters? You can never trust them." She took a step toward Allister, a mean gleam in her eyes. "The only good vampire is a dead one."

Allister tensed as if to attack.

I scrambled for something to say. Something to ease the tension. "Is that all you came for? To return my weapons and interrogate me? If so, you're done. I haven't broken any of my part. I protected Allister, but no one else."

Mizuki's glare didn't waver from Allister. "Haven't you wondered why we were at the club at all? Who tipped us off?"

I didn't answer. She knew I had.

She stepped closer to Allister, so they were barely a breath away from each other. "Someone has been very sloppy with their victims."

"They aren't victims if they're willing," Allister replied, the tension in his body rising.

"Anyone you sink your fangs into is a victim. Whether they see it that way or not."

"Enough of the cock tease, Mizuki," I snapped, getting tired of the cryptic. "What's going on?"

Mizuki finally looked away from Allister and stepped back to meet my questioning gaze. "There have been ten murders, all of them female. All of them blood whores who frequented Club Dead."

"And did you get the vampire responsible?" I prodded, hoping that the inkling in the back of my head wasn't what I thought it was.

"No. We didn't." Mizuki turned that intense glare back to Allister.

Allister frowned. "You can't think I did it?"

"What proof do you have?" I pushed myself between them, knowing I only had my dagger if it came down to a fight. If I was quick, I could grab my gun, but that's only if I could do it before Mizuki got to him.

Mizuki stared over my head at Allister until I waved a hand in her face. "Hello? You can't just come into our house and make accusations. Do you have any proof?"

"No," Mizuki looked at me. "If you hadn't bolted from the fight, you would have been there to get it as well."

My stomach was in my throat as I asked, "Well, where is it?"

"The bartender claims several of the victims were seen with your vampire on the nights they were murdered." Mizuki's blood-red lips curled up into a cruel smile.

Allister moved behind me, and I held a hand up to stop him. "That's not proof. That's a coincidence, at best."

"Proof enough. We've killed vampires for less."

Allister snorted. "Yeah. Like existing."

"It's our way."

Mizuki moved closer, so I was pressed between the two of them. I couldn't get to my dagger, but I could almost reach my gun. Darren saw what I was going for and pushed the gun closer to me. I grabbed hold of it and pressed it to her stomach.

Mizuki froze.

"Back off," I demanded through clenched teeth.

"You dare to betray us?" Mizuki looked away from Allister to survey me.

I barked a laugh. "I'm not the one here using this sham to try and kill one of my guys. If anyone is the traitor, it is you."

"He's a vampire. What other proof do you need?" Mizuki moved her attention back to Allister, forgetting all about me. Big mistake.

Not wanting to kill her if I didn't have to, I shoved her away and then swiped my foot behind her knee, bringing her to the ground. I placed a foot on her chest and aimed for her face before she could react.

"You forget, Mizuki," I seethe, my finger itching to pull the trigger. "I'm not one of you. I'm one of them. So, unless you have more proof than that, I suggest you leave. Or do I need to bring this up with Vincent?"

Mizuki studied me for a moment. "You wouldn't do it. You're too human to kill another of your kind."

I took the safety off and cocked the gun, lining up the shot. "We are not the same."

"What's going on here?" A voice from the kitchen doorway distracted me. It was enough time for Mizuki to pull one of her own blades and drive it into my leg.

"Shit!" I screamed and went down, giving Mizuki enough time to get out from under me. She didn't try to attack me or anyone else. She was just gone.

"Fucking hell, Piper!" Jack Biggs knelt at my side, his face pale. "She stabbed you."

"Yeah," I let out a painful laugh. "She did."

Darren moved across the room, probably headed for the first aid kit while Jack freaked out.

"We can't just let her get away. I'll call the cops. An ambulance." Jack moved to get off the ground, but Allister stopped him.

"She'll be fine."

"What? Are you crazy? She's bleeding out here?" Jack tried to pull out his phone. Allister's hand landed on top of his, and he said once more, "Piper is fine. Go back to your room and forget about everything you saw here today."

I shivered against the feel of Allister's power on my skin. They didn't say he had a silver tongue for nothing.

Jack stared blankly at Allister for a long moment and then nodded. "Piper's fine. I'm going to go back to my room."

"Good. You do that." Allister smacked him on the cheek lightly before pushing him toward the door.

Jack walked stiffly out of the room. Drake walked in after him. He watched Jack leave and then saw me bleeding on the floor. "What's up with the Big Man? And what'd you do, Piper? Walk into a knife?"

I looked up at him and winced. "Haha. You're hilarious." I shifted back until I could lean against the wall as Darren knelt before me. "Mizuki did it."

Drake sucked in a breath. "What? And you just let her go?" He stalked across the room and headed for the door. Allister stopped him. "Don't just stand there."

"This is going to hurt," Darren said, drawing my attention back to him before he wrapped his hand around the knife's handle. I braced myself, looking up at Allister to see him shake his head at his brother. "Don't."

I bit back a scream as Darren pulled the knife from my leg.

A rush of footsteps poured into the kitchen. Rayne and Marcus appeared in the doorway. They took one look at me and then the blood flowing from my wound. Rayne rushed over to the fridge and grabbed his silver container of blood before disappearing back into the dining room. Marcus stayed, his nostrils flaring, but he made no move to leave or feed.

"What happened?" Marcus asked.

I leaned my head back against the wall. "Can we save the explanations for after I don't bleed to death?"

"Here." Marcus lowered himself to my side, slashing his wrist with a single nail before holding it out to me. "Drink. You'll heal."

I groaned and reached out for his arm. "I'm not going to get any sleep this week, am I?" Lowering my mouth to his wrist, I sucked down the thick coppery liquid, swallowing until my leg didn't throb quite so much. "Enough," I pushed his arm away and turned my head the other way.

"You're not completely healed," Drake complained, leaning against the kitchen island. "You'll scar."

I looked up at Drake and scowled. "I'll live."

"I would like answers now." Marcus hovered at my side. "Who did this to you?"

"Don't worry about it." I pushed up off the floor and swayed, Darren and Marcus both reached for me at the same time. "I'm good." I shook them off and then inched up until I could sit at the table instead of on the floor.

"I will worry about it." Marcus loomed over me. "If someone has attacked you, they have declared war on our family. I must know who it is."

"Where's Antoine?" I ignored his question and turned to Darren.

"He went to shower. Do you want me to fetch him?" Darren moved to go, but I caught his hand.

That's why he hadn't come running at the commotion like the others. A vampire's hearing had limits. "No. Stay." I smiled weakly up at him. "Rayne will get him." While Rayne might not be able to handle so much of my blood at once without feeding, I knew he wouldn't be too far away. At my words, there were footsteps on the staircase, and then a door slammed somewhere.

"Tell us," Drake insisted. "Have the hunters finally turned on us? Do we need to go into hiding again?"

I waved him off. "I'm not going to repeat myself. Wait." To Darren, I asked, "Can I get some water?"

Darren nodded and moved over to the kitchen. No doubt doing more than I asked of him.

It didn't take long for Rayne to return with Antoine close behind him. The master vampire had barely gotten dressed, let alone dry his hair. The white strands of his hair were almost gray from being wet as it soaked into the silk of his button down shirt. Antoine took one look at me, and the blood drying on my calf and snarled.

"I'll kill them."

"Stop," I called out to him, "wait. Don't go doing anything rash. I'm fine." Darren placed a cup of tea on the table before me. I gave him a look, but he pushed the cup closer, urging me to take it. Sighing in defeat, I was too tired to argue anyway, I picked up the cup and took a small sip. Grimacing at the taste, I sat it back down to look at the vampires in the room. "We have a problem."

"Obviously." Drake laughed darkly. "The hunters need to die."

"That's not the problem. I mean, yes, they do eventually," I explained, my gaze sliding over to Allister. "Allister? Tell me what Mizuki said wasn't true? You didn't kill those women, did you?"

Allister stiffened on his side of the room, having been quiet the entire time.

"What?" Antoine looked to Allister, a quiet rage on his face.

"Please tell me this isn't true." Wynn appeared in the kitchen doorway. "Sorry, I'm late, love." He wiped the side of his mouth as if he had just finished eating, then his dark blue orbs glared at Allister. "Please tell me you haven't put us all in danger for a fit of childish jealousy."

"You knew?" I shot a look at Wynn, betrayal stinging in my heart. "You knew he was going out to that club every night with another girl, and you didn't say anything?"

Wynn held his hands out to his sides and gave me a pleading look. "My apologies, pet. It was not my place to tell. Allister was supposed to work through his issues and talk to you. It is not my fault he did not do so."

"And the rest of you?" I glanced around the room, looking for someone else with a guilty face. "Did you know?"

Drake shook his head. "No. I didn't. Fucking hell. Allister. I'm your brother. Your twin, and you kept this from me?"

Allister didn't respond, determined it seemed to keep quiet.

"I knew." Rayne lifted a finger in the air. "Or at least part of it." He gave a guilty shrug. "I try to stay out of their minds if I can help it, but some thoughts are louder than others."

"So, you knew he was going out every night?" I prodded, trying to find out the depth of his knowledge.

Shaking his redhead, Rayne said, "No. No. I didn't know about that. Just that he was feeling a bit neglected."

I huffed a laugh. "Neglected. Huh. Well, Allister's neglected feelings have now put us in some very deep shit. Haven't they?" I locked my eyes on the larger vampire.

"Piper," Marcus placed a hand on my shoulder. "Tell us what has happened."

Staring at Allister, I tried to control my emotions. "I had a call to Club Dead today, as you know. They were looking for a vampire who was going on a killing spree and wasn't being very clever about it. Ten girls in the span of ten nights. Each one someone the bartender said was with Allister the same night at the club."

The others all looked to Allister at that moment. The mixture of emotions on their faces equaled to that of my own. Anger. Horror. Disbelief. Sadness. Had he really done it? Had Allister, sweet, quiet Allister, really killed all those women? I couldn't believe it. I wouldn't, not without proof—more than just some bartender's word.

"Well, Allister," Antoine finally asked, his voice void of any emotion. "What do you have to say for yourself?"

Allister locked eyes with me, not looking at anyone else in the room, and said, "It's true. I was with those women."

CHAPTER 14
Marcus

"OF ALL OF MY brothers, you were not the one I thought would damn us all." I leaned against the wall next to Piper. She said she was fine, but Piper always said she was fine. I didn't trust her to tell us the truth about her own wellbeing.

"My money had been on Rayne," Drake smirked at the hot-headed vampire. "God knows he puts his nose in where it doesn't belong enough."

Rayne glared at Drake. "And if I'd listened a little harder, maybe we wouldn't be in this mess."

"We don't even know exactly what mess we are in," Drake pointed out, pushing up off the kitchen island. "So, fess up, brother. Did you knock off these broads or what?"

"Drake," Piper gaped at him and shook her head. The movement made her groan and lower her head to the table. "I think I'm going to be sick."

"You should go lay down," Darren placed a hand on top of hers.

Piper pulled her hand away and lifted her head. "No. Not until we figure this out."

"Fine. Then let's figure this out." Drake turned his twin. "Well? Did you?"

Allister rubbed the back of his head and laughed harshly. "How can you even ask that?"

"Well, *mon ami*?" Wynn glanced up from his place against the fridge. "Answer the question."

Allister's form stiffened, his gaze growing hard. "No. I did not kill those women. Happy?"

"No," Drake snapped. "What would make me happy is if you hadn't gotten the hunters' attention at all!"

"Calm yourself," I shifted away from the wall as Drake made for his twin. "We do not need to fight amongst ourselves on top of everything."

"What he said," Piper muttered into the table, lifting an arm in the air.

Antoine smoothed his hands over his clothing and stepped up to Allister. "You have put this entire family at risk." Allister's face dropped at Antoine's words. "You must right this wrong before the hunters cannot be convinced otherwise."

"How am I supposed to do that?"

"Marcus." Antoine gestured to me without turning.

"Yes." I stepped toward him, ready to do my duty.

"You have more experience in things of this nature. You will assist Allister in this task." Piper made a grunt of protest, and Antoine sighed reluctantly. "Piper will join you once she has eaten and slept." Piper made a sound as if to argue, but Antoine was firm. "I will not have you passing out somewhere that we will not be able to help you. Let us take care of the matter. You keep yourself from earning the ire of any more hunters."

I cleared my throat, gaining Antoine's attention.

"Oh, yes. There is also the matter of your human." Antoine turned away from Allister, clearly dismissing him. "Tonight was close. Too close. He needs to be gone...today."

Piper lifted her head from the table finally. "Just command him gone or something. Geez. You act like you don't use your powers for everything as it is."

Antoine arched a brow. "I was under the impression you did not wish me to use my abilities on your friends."

My lips twitched at his words. Calling Jack Biggs Piper's friend was putting it nicely. The man was a lawyer. He might have initially come out of concern for Piper, but he could smell a secret a mile away. I had come across enough lawyers in my time that I knew to steer clear of them.

Piper collapsed back on the table with a dramatic sigh. "At this point, I don't care. Just get rid of him."

"Come on, Piper." Darren stood and took her by the arm, helping her stand. "Let's get you to bed. Leave the complications for the masters."

Piper snorted, leaning into Darren's arms. "Some masters can't even keep their fangs in their mouth long enough not to get us killed."

Allister growled at Piper as she passed. She patted him on the butt, making him jump. "Just don't get us killed. Okay, Al?"

"Don't call me that," Allister quipped but didn't have any anger behind it.

We waited for Piper to reach the top of the stairs before the discussion began again. There were many concerns with what we should do to prove Allister's innocence. None of them protested more than Allister himself.

"This is pointless. We can't even go check the club out until after dark. We should all just go to bed and deal with this when the sun goes down." Allister threw himself into a chair at the kitchen table and slammed his hand down on the top of it. "What the fuck was Benny thinking?"

"Benny?" Rayne asked. "The bartender?"

"Yeah," Allister grumbled, rubbing a finger between his brows.

Rayne snorted in disbelief. "You're on a first-name basis with the bartender? You really have been going there too much."

Allister stared hard down at the ground.

The younger vampire barked a laugh. "Seriously? You thought those bimbos would make you feel better? Idiot."

"Stay out of my head," Allister snapped at Rayne, slamming his hand down on the table again. "What I was doing there is none of your business."

"It is if your decisions affect this family." Drake stalked over to his brother and grabbed him by the front of his shirt, lifting him up from his seat. "Especially if they hurt Piper. How could you do that to her?"

Allister jerked away from his brother's hands and shoved back up from the table. "I've already taken care of it. And I wasn't doing anything you're thinking of. So, just fuck off."

Drake glanced over at Rayne, who shrugged. "He's telling the truth. He only talked to them after he fed."

"Obviously, you spent too much time with these women, or the bartender wouldn't have remembered you being with them," I pointed out, crossing my arms over my chest. "When we left Bulgaria to form our own household, we made a promise to each other. A promise to protect this family. How are your actions upholding that promise?"

Allister dragged a hand over his face and sighed. "I never intended it to get that far. It was just one time, and then the next thing I know, I'm in this cluster fuck. Look. I know I fucked up. Now, instead of berating me about it, why don't we come up with a solution to figure out who actually killed those women?"

"Young Allister has a point." Wynn mused, pushing away from the fridge. "Arguing amongst ourselves will get us nowhere. We must retire for the day. Antione," he paused until he gained our leader's attention. "Can you reach out to Morpheus? See if he has anything to say about this? It would be a sad coincidence indeed that he would be saved by us only to have one of our own be punished for someone else in his club's mistakes."

Antoine inclined his head. "Agreed. The timing is too precise to be just fate." He walked to the doorway of the kitchen. "I will make my inquiries, and I too will retire for the day."

I cleared my throat. "What of the human?"

Our leader stopped at the doorway. "Ah, yes." He sighed as if it was all catching up to him, and it was just too much. "I suppose I will be stopping by Mr. Biggs's room on the way to bed as well. Good day, brothers."

We muttered our good days in response. Then we went off to do our assigned tasks. Allister to make a list of all the women he spent the evening with and what time he left each of them. Rayne would cross-reference the times he left with the times he returned home on the security system here at the house. One thing for modern technology, it made it much easier to prove someone's innocence or their guilt. I could have used a camera or two on my crusades. It would have made my life easier for sure.

Drake followed his twin, either to help him or to give him shit for putting us all in such a predicament. Wynn went to do whatever he did to help. After centuries by his side, I had stopped asking. Usually, it wasn't an answer I wanted to know.

I found myself sitting in the kitchen when Darren returned. He walked through the kitchen as if I didn't exist. Only when Darren pulled down two mugs from the cabinet and filled them both with coffee did he even show that he knew I was there. He brought the cup to me. The liquid inside, blacker than my eyes. After all these years, Darren had done well to remember our preferences.

"Thank you." I wrapped my hands around the mug, breathing in the scent without taking a sip. "How is she?"

Darren sat across from me at the table and sipped from his coffee mug. "Tired. She's suffered a lot of blood loss lately, not counting all the beatings she has sustained. I think it's catching up with her."

I hummed. "Yes, she does seem to keep going even when on empty."

"Stubbornness will be her fall one of these days."

Lifting my mug to my lips, I gulped a mouthful of hot liquid. "I do not know what we are going to do with her. I sometimes wonder why Antoine even bothered with a human servant." Darren didn't take offense to my comment and simply listened. "They were just inconveniences. Or someone to clean up after us. We could have paid people to do that. Why keep someone who you'd be stuck with forever?"

Darren nodded. I didn't know if he agreed with me or was just being a good listener.

"Then, there's Piper." I held the cup between both of my hands tight enough that the heat of the mug was beginning to get uncomfortable. "I didn't want her here either. She was an even bigger inconvenience. No offense meant." Darren waved me off. "She's loud. Rude. Sticks her nose in where it doesn't belong." I chuckled. "And she attracts too much attention. Good and bad."

"That she does," Darren murmured.

"She's so strong. So much stronger than I gave her credit for." I sighed and lowered my head over my cup. "I always thought to be strong, you had to be physically strong. Be the better monster. I forgot about being strong...in here." I touched my chest with an open palm. I'd give up all my strength to be even half as strong as her."

Darren didn't say anything.

I thought he might not have been listening, but when I lifted my head, I saw him staring off to the side where Piper was standing by the stairs.

I cleared my throat and shifted in my seat. "Shouldn't you be resting?"

Piper smiled softly and walked over to me. "I wanted something to eat. Then I heard your little speech."

Ducking my head, I felt my face warm. Was I blushing? I never blushed. What was this woman doing to me?

"You know," Piper moved over to me, sliding her arms around my shoulders. "I think that's the most I've ever heard you talk...like, ever." She giggled and leaned into me, placing her head on top of mine. "Thank you, Marcus. I really needed to hear that."

I placed my hand on top of her arm. "You're welcome."

CHAPTER 15
Piper

I SHOULD HAVE KNOWN drinking blood from not one but two vampires in less than a twenty-four-hour period was going to be bad for my sleep. In any other circumstance, I wouldn't have minded. Most of the time, my vampire blood dreams were orgasmic, and I wouldn't say no to that kind of stress relief.

Not today, though.

Today, I wanted a dark nothingness. To my dismay, that's not what I got.

It was interesting to be dreaming of Allister and Marcus, the two vampires I'd taken blood from. Usually, Antoine and Rayne were the ones to donate to me. With Allister causing all kinds of havoc for the family, I didn't particularly want to be dreaming of him. Dreaming of Marcus doing naughty things to the insides of my thighs when we'd only ever kissed was all kinds of awkward.

"I can't," dream me breathed heavily, hands gripping Allister's hands above me as Marcus devoured me from below. "No more. Please."

"Yes," Allister purred in my ear, his smooth-talking tongue causing my skin to peddle with need. "You want more."

Marcus pulled my clit between his fangs, sucking it into his mouth hard and fast. My spine bowed, and I screamed my release.

Jerking up, I opened my eyes to find myself alone in my bed—no Marcus or Allister in sight. Breathing heavily, I waited until my body calmed, but my pulse was still pounding between my legs from my release. God, I hoped no one heard me.

The chances no one heard me screaming were slim to none, and I waited to see who would come running. After about five minutes and no one appearing, I frowned, sliding from my bed. I padded across the room and ducked my head out of the bedroom door. The hallways were empty. I angled my head to the side, listening with my enhanced hearing for some form of life in the house.

The kitchen.

Sniffing the air tentatively, I caught a whiff of apple pie and not just anyone's apple pie but Gretchen's famous melt in your mouth apple pie.

Mouthwatering, I shut the door and hurried into my clothes. I pulled on a pair of jeans and a black V-neck shirt with little cherries all over it. A quick glance at the clock told me I'd been asleep most of the day. It was already three in the afternoon. Which made me wonder where the hell the rest of the household was? Were they sleeping? Or did they try to venture out to find out who was trying to frame Allister?

Shoving my cell phone into my back pocket, I pulled my tennis shoes on and headed for the door. In the hallway, I started towards the servant's stairs when another door opened. Thinking it was one of the guys, I turned a smile on my face. What faced me promptly squashed that smile.

"Jack, I thought you went home already?" I walked toward the lawyer, my mind whirling. Why hadn't Antoine gotten rid of him yet?

He was dressed in his work best, which was unusual for traveling. Even a social visit. What was going on?

Jack's gaze skimmed over my form, a small smile sliding up his face. "Oh, yes. Well, something came up. Your boyfriend? Boss?" He chuckled and shook his head. "Whatever he is to you, has requested my assistance with an issue he was having. So, I decided to stick around for a little while."

My frown only deepened. What the hell was Antoine thinking?

"That's okay, right?" Jack seemed to sense my unease. "Because if it's not, I can call a colleague of mine and have them handle it."

"No, no." I blew out a breath and forced myself to relax. "If Antoine thinks it's fine, then I trust his judgment." Part of the time anyway. "I was just going to head down and see if I could steal some pie from our cook, Gretchen. Do you want to come?"

Jack's smile spread, but he held up his hands. "Sadly, I'll have to pass. I have some papers to go over with Mr. Durand before work hours are over." He paused and tilted his head slightly. It was that boy next door charm kind of face that I'd seen him use several times on prospective clients. Why he was using it on me made me nervous. "Rain check?"

I tried to keep my face neutral as I studied him. "Uh, yeah. Sure. See you."

Watching Jack as he headed toward Antoine's office, I was half tempted to follow him and listen in at the door. Which would have been stupid since Antoine would have sensed me in a heartbeat. Reluctantly, I left it alone and headed for the kitchen. I'd get an explanation eventually, even if it wasn't when I wanted it.

"Ah, there she is." Gretchen greeted me, a motherly grin on her face and flour all over her apron. "I was beginning to think you would sleep all day."

I rounded the kitchen island and hugged the older woman. Her plump figure pressed against me and filled my nose with her scent. Butter and cinnamon. I kind of thought of Gretchen like my own mother or maybe grandmother. I wasn't sure how she'd feel about the latter, so I never mentioned it. My own mother was a piece of work that Antoine had thankfully gotten to leave me alone after a surprise visit. My parents were a lot of things, but loving wasn't one of them. Definitely not domestic like Gretchen.

"Sorry, I had a long night." I released her and moved around the kitchen in search of coffee.

"So I heard," Gretchen mused, arching a brow at me. "You're going to run yourself ragged if you don't take care of yourself."

Once I had my hands on a cup of coffee, I sighed and leaned against the kitchen counter. "Believe me. I'm not doing it on purpose. Everything just keeps piling up on top of each other."

"So I've been told." Gretchen returned to the stove, where she checked the pie in the oven. "From maid to vampire hunter, and now you have this whole business with Master Allister to worry about." She clucked her tongue like a worrying hen. "Not to mention the handsome lawyer sticking his nose about."

I frowned, mid-sip of coffee. "Jack?"

"Yes," Gretchen nodded, grabbing an oven mitt from the counter. "Master Antoine was beside himself when he came down earlier, muttering things about no good rotten lawyers. And something not quite so pleasant I wouldn't repeat to you." She smiled, and I grinned back.

"Did Antoine happen to mention why he hadn't sent Jack away?" I finally sipped from my coffee cup and waited for what I hoped was a rational response.

Before Gretchen could answer, the timer on the stovetop went off. She set about opening the oven and pulling out the apple pie. Gretchen sat it on the cooling rack set up next to the stove and turned back to me. "He didn't say. However, I suspect it has something to do with the fact that the properties he'd had his eyes on recently were all snatched up from under his nose."

My brows drew together. "What does that have to do with anything? It's not like he doesn't have other properties and businesses to worry about."

Gretchen inclined her head. "Of course, but that was until he found out that the companies he was planning on taking apart and selling off to the highest bidder were suddenly bankrupt."

My eyes widened, and my mouth gaped open. I placed my coffee cup down on the counter before I dropped it and stared at her. "How is this possible? Companies don't go bankrupt overnight?"

Lifting a shoulder and dropping it, Gretchen went about getting plates down from the cabinet. "Don't ask me. I have no mind for business. And all this is secondhand information."

Curiosity filled me, and a thought came. "Who exactly gave you this knowledge? I know Darren isn't that much of a busy body. And Antoine certainly wouldn't offer up the information on his own." I took a step toward her, a mischievous grin playing on my lips. "Who did you get to spill their guts, and how?"

Gretchen gave me a sideways look, and a tiny secretive grin played on her lips. "You didn't think after being with this family for so long that I didn't figure out ways to get information, did you?"

I laughed and bumped her on the shoulder. "Come on, tell me. Who is the sucker? And what did you feed them?"

Placing a hand on her hip, Gretchen stared at me incredulously. "What makes you think I fed them anything? Couldn't it have been my womanly charms that made them talk?"

I arched a brow.

"Fine." She huffed. "It was Drake. And about four of these pies." She pointed at the apple pie on the cooling rack. "That boy is a sucker for a good fruit pie. I swear you'd think it was blood the way he sucked them down."

Chuckling to myself at the image, I put that knowledge away for later. My laughter died as I realized the predicament we were all in. How much of a coincidence was it that Allister is suspected of murder and they were having business issues? Too big of one to ignore.

"Save me a slice of pie," I told Gretchen, touching her on the shoulder as I passed by. I had to get to the bottom of this. Someone was fucking with us, and I wanted to know who and why.

"No promises," Gretchen called after me.

I stepped into the dining room and considered my options. Antoine was upstairs with Jack handling whatever was going on with the businesses, no doubt. It was pure luck that Jack was here when we needed a lawyer. Especially one with his rate of cases won. Jack Biggs might be full of himself, but he had good reason to be. Jack had won enough cases against big corporate companies trying to screw the little man to be able to handle Antoine's accounts.. So, that left the rest of us to help Allister.

Turning to the door in the dining room that leads to the basement, I stopped before it. My hand hesitated over the doorknob. The basement had been one secret the Durands had kept from me even after they had let me into their hearts and put myself into servitude for them. It was the one thing keeping me from being completely one of them. Darren had been down there. In fact, he was the one who cleaned it when I had been the one cleaning the house. And he wasn't even sleeping with any of them. Or well, I guess Antoine, but I still outnumbered him on the number of Durands I had in my bed. I had every right to be down there.

Yeah. I did. No reason to be nervous. It wasn't like they slept in coffins. Even Darren told me that was dumb. No. It was just where they slept—no big deal.

My fingers curled around the doorknob and turned. It clicked open. My breath flew out of me in a rush. I didn't know why I thought they would lock the door to me now. In fact, I hadn't tried to go in there since before we went into hiding. I stepped into the doorway at the top of the stairs and frowned. Actually, they should have locked it with a stranger in our home. Jack could have easily come in here and walked in on them doing

God knows what they did down there. Vampire blood orgy?

"Are you going to stand there all day or come down?" Rayne called, poking his head around the corner at the bottom of the stairs.

Pursing my lips, I made my way down the stairs until I landed in front of him. "You know, you should really lock that door with Jack in the house," I told him with a frown.

Rayne smirked at me. "What do you think he's going to find, a vampire blood orgy?"

I scoffed and bumped him with my elbow. "Stay out of my head, doofus."

"I'll stay out of your head when you stop projecting so hard." Rayne slid his arm around my waist and leaned in to press his lips against the bend of my neck. "Your dreams were quite interesting to read as well."

I rolled my eyes and pushed him away from me. "Of course they were. I had vampire blood for dinner."

"Interesting dreams?" Wynn mused from one of the twin beds lined along each side of the wall. A couch sat in front of a big-screen television where the twins sat arguing over a football game.

My nose crinkled up, and my eyes squinted. "It's just so...ordinary."

"What were you expecting?" Drake called over his shoulder, sucking down some dark red liquid in a glass with a straw. "Coffins and Dracula brides?"

I snorted. "If anyone has brides, it's me." Rayne covered up a laugh beside me with a cough. "So, what are we doing about Allister's dead blood whores?"

Wynn arched a brow, laying his legs out in front of him on the bed. "Someone is still a bit jealous."

Frowning at him, I crossed my arms over my chest and glowered at him. "I am not."

Rayne kissed me on the cheek. "Are too."

I swatted at him and stalked through the room. "My jealousy is beside the point. I need answers. Please tell me you've done something other than fuck around in here all day?"

CHAPTER 16
Wynn

JEALOUSY BECAME PIPER. IT wasn't typically something I found attractive in a woman. Most of the time, it was irritating. Now, I found it utterly charming. Even though her jealousy had nothing to do with me.

"And what pray tell, did you expect us to do? " I crossed one leg over the other, leaning back against my headboard. "The sun shines, and we can do nothing until it has set. You, on the other hand, are not bound by our restrictions."

"Yeah, yeah. Human servant and all that jazz." Piper plopped down on the side of my bed and fiddled with my sleeve. I liked that she wanted to be near me without me having to ask. I wrapped my arm around her waist and drew her up the bed beside me. She snuggled into my embrace and played with the buttons of my shirt. Glancing up at me, she cocked her head to the side. "However, I don't even know where to start. Who would want to frame Allister? And what's all this stuff about the businesses having issues?"

I frowned down at her. "And how do you know of our financial issues? We haven't known very long ourselves. You certainly shouldn't have known yet."

"Gretchen told her," Rayne sat on the end of my bed, his brows drawn together as he stared at Piper and then over at Drake. "Someone needs to knock off the pies."

"Hey," Drake called out from the couch. "I have very few things left in this world I can enjoy. Leave me alone about the pies."

Rayne snorted. "Yeah, well, when you are talking about our private business with the help, then it's a problem."

I felt Piper stiffen against me. Stroking my fingers along her bare arm, I leaned my head down to her ear. "I'm sure Rayne doesn't mean it like that, love."

Piper didn't relax at my words. "I know I don't really work for you guys anymore, but I don't like to think you'd talk about Gretchen that way. I mean, she's been with you for longer than I have, and she doesn't deserve that."

"You're right." Rayne placed his hand on Piper's thigh next to him. "I'm sorry. I didn't mean to be so abrupt about it. Gretchen has proven her loyalty ten times over."

"I believe what our Rayne is trying to say," I smoothed my hand over her cheek and turned her gaze to mine, "is that we are all on edge right now. None of us expected any of this to happen."

Allister scoffed. "That's for sure. It's getting to be that a vampire can't get a drink anymore without getting brought up for murder."

"Well, if you kept your fangs to yourself and drank from the blood provided, then you wouldn't have that problem, now would you?" Piper snipped back, glowering at Allister, who shifted on the couch to look at her.

"I thought you forgave me?"

Piper crossed her arms over her chest and turned slightly away from all of us. "That was before I heard about the nine other women. I can't believe you!" She stood up and stalked across the room. "And don't tell me that it's because you were feeling neglected. There are six other guys in this house, and you don't see any of them going out and making blood eyes at anyone that will have them?"

"Oh, so we're all supposed to just be monogamous to you, but you can be with all of us?" Allister jumped up and over the couch.

"Careful, brother," I cautioned. Things could quickly spiral out of control if he did not watch his words. Our happy arrangement had been going well without him rocking the boat, so to speak.

"What?" Allister shot a glare my way. "I'm just saying what everyone else is thinking. Can't tell me none of you have thought how unfair this all is?" He gestured at Piper, his lip curling up in a sneer.

Piper glanced around the room, her eyes wide. She licked her lips and cleared her throat. "Is he right? Do you all think that?"

"What?" Rayne came up behind her, placing his hands on her shoulders.

Piper jerked away from him. "No, don't touch me. Do you really think that? Am I being unfair?"

"No, of course not." Rayne tried to follow after her. "There's no one else I want to be with than you."

"Not now, maybe." Piper swallowed and shook her head. "But who knows later, you might find some girl that you want to sink your teeth into and think like Allister. That why shouldn't you get to have her too? I mean, I'm doing the lot of you, what do you owe me?"

Oh, dear. This was what I was afraid of. Allister's misspoken words had sent us down a spiral of what-ifs and maybes. There was only one person who could fix this—the one who started it.

"Pet," I stood from the bed and approached her slowly as one would do a jittery deer, "please do not take Allister's words for what the rest of us are feeling. He speaks from a place of anger and perhaps a bit of guilt." I glanced Allister's way. He simply growled in response.

"Yeah, Piper." Drake threw an arm over the couch and pouted up at her. "Don't let my bone head twin make you feel bad about yourself. He's the one in the wrong, not you.

Believe me, we're going to be giving him hell about this for the next century." He shot a glare at his brother.

Allister returned his brother's glare with one of his own. "I have done nothing to earn such ire from you, Draconius."

"And yet, here we are?" Drake snapped, baring his fangs. "We are in this mess because of you. If you'd just unwadded your panties and used your words to tell Piper how you felt, then maybe we wouldn't be trying to keep the hunters from killing you. Do you have any idea what kind of position you've put her in? You could have not only gotten yourself killed but her and the rest of us. Is that worth your hurt feelings?"

Allister shifted in place for a moment, his gaze off to the side. Finally, he sighed and dropped his arms to his side. "No. It's not. And really," he looked up to Piper with a painful expression, "I don't think it's unfair. I don't want anyone else. I just want you."

Piper pulled her lower lip in between her teeth. It was clear she wasn't sure how to respond to Allister's words. Trying to help the matter along, I slid an arm around her shoulders and pressed my forehead to the side of her face, murmuring, "Just be honest."

She shifted her head toward me and huffed a laugh. "Now you tell me."

We waited for her to gather her thoughts. Finally, Piper threw her hands up and stepped toward Allister. "I don't know how to do this. They didn't exactly cover how to date multiple guys at once in health class." Piper gave a weak smile. "I don't know how to make everyone feel wanted and not have this," she gestured to Allister, "happen again." Letting out a bitter laugh, Piper shook her head. "Hell, before you all, I hadn't kept a solid boyfriend for more than a few months. Definitely not one that would last longer than my lifetime."

Allister took a step toward her, timid as he reached for her. "I don't think any of us really know what we are doing, either."

"That's why communication is important," Rayne pointed out. "You can't just assume anything, or you're going to end up in situations like this."

"Easy for you to say," Allister scowled. "You can just read our minds and know what's wrong. The rest of us have to figure out the right words to say, and sometimes we don't even realize why we're doing something until we've already gone and made an ass out of ourselves."

Piper threw her head back and laughed, one of the most beautiful sounds I'd ever heard. "Okay, alright. We all need to work on our communication skills." She closed the distance between her and Allister, lifting a hand and sliding her finger up and down along the opening of his ripped tank top. "I'll try and make sure to make time for all of you, and you have to tell me when you are feeling neglected."

Allister nodded. "Agreed."

"No more blood whores then?" Piper arched a brow. Her face made her seem like she was teasing. Still, the tension in her shoulders told me how worried she was about Allister actually keeping up with his debauchery.

Lifting a hand to bump underneath Piper's chin, Allister leaned forward and pressed a chaste kiss to her lips. "No more blood whores."

Piper jerked her head once and then spun around. "And that goes for the rest of you. If you can drink from blood containers rather than blood donors, I ask that you do so. Don't think I don't know that taking blood is just as close to sex for you and the person donating." She pointed a knowing finger around the room.

"So..." I purred, stalking across the room. "You're saying that you are the only one we are allowed to bite?"

Piper's lovely face turned a delicious shade of red as she shifted in place. "Well, uh, I suppose I am."

Stroking a finger along where her pulse sat, the blood beneath thudding even faster as my touch. "I do believe I can accept those terms. And what about the rest of you? Do you find this demand unacceptable?"

"No complaints here," Rayne answered.

Drake jumped over the couch and bounded over to us with a wide grin. "Oh, hell no. I've been dying to sink my fangs into you and something else, too, if you catch my drift." He wagged his brows suggestively in Piper's direction.

"I guess I can't really say no," Allister shoved his hands into his gym shorts. Piper shot him a look, and he smiled. "I'm teasing. I'm good with it."

"Well, you don't have to worry about Antoine swaying. He only drinks from you and Darren as it is," Rayne flipped his red hair out of his face. "I'm assuming that is alright with you?" He looked to Piper expectantly.

Piper shrugged. "I mean if you want to drink each other's blood. You could do that, but I mean, I didn't think that actually did anything for you nutritionally."

"No, not really." Drake shrugged a shoulder. "Some do it during sex, but it's a bit like eating your own arm. Yeah, it fills your stomach, but it doesn't do you any good if you don't have an arm, you know?"

"Uh...yeah." Piper glanced away from him and asked us, "So what are we going to do about whoever is trying to ruin our lives?"

"Pardon?" I frowned at her, my brothers' expressions showing just as much confusion.

"Oh, come on." Piper huffed. "You can't believe this is all coincidence, do you?" She peered around the room. "I mean, Allister being framed, the businesses going under, and even Jack's convenient appearance? Someone is fucking with us. The only question is, who?"

An awful feeling came over me, and I couldn't hold back my horror. "I think I know who."

Rayne snorted. "No way. He doesn't have that much pull. I mean, come on. He wants an excuse to sink his teeth into Piper again, but he wouldn't go this far." I just stared at him. "This is ridiculous. It doesn't make sense."

"To him, it might," I explained, willing him to see it another way.

Piper's head jerked from me to Rayne. "Would one of you tell me what is going on? Who's out to get us? And what do you mean, sink their fangs into me?" She grabbed the side of her neck, and her face paled. "Not Valentine? We killed him. He can't be back. Can he?"

"No, no, my love." I cupped her face and pulled her close. "Vampires can do many things but coming back from true death is not one of them."

"Then who is it?" Piper peered up at me, the fear still on the edges of her gaze.

"Isn't it obvious?" I smoothed my thumb across her cheek. "Who gains much from eradicating our family from Georgia? Who becomes the most powerful vampire in the whole region?" I paused for a moment, waiting to see if they had come to their own conclusions.

It was Piper who figured it out first. Her eyes hardened, and her jaw clenched as she bit out, "Morpheus."

CHAPTER 17
Piper

I WAS GOING TO kill Morpheus. I was going to find that smug little prick, pull him limb from limb, starting with his smallest, most favorite one. Then, I was going to rip out his heart and grind it into dust, mix it with my morning coffee, and drink what is left of Morpheus, the mother fucking vampire. Maybe I'll even wear his fangs as a pair of earrings. Yeah. That would make an excellent threat to the other vampires in this state.

"Geez, Piper," Rayne's lip curled up in a grimace. "Nice visual."

I flushed. "Sorry."

"So, Morpheus is an asshole," Drake growled, "Why am I not surprised?"

"Well, sitting down here isn't going to fix any of this." Allister dragged a hand over his face. "We need to find Morpheus and make him fess up. Fix whatever he did to the businesses. Or the vampire hunters are not going to be the worst of our problems."

I winced. "Yeah. I probably need to smooth things over with them." I suddenly had a thought. I pulled my cell out of my back pocket and sighed. Yep. Several missed calls from one Vincent, vampire hunter president, and pain in my ass. Fuck. This wasn't going to be fun. "I need to see the president. Maybe I can get them to sniff around for Morpheus."

"Any luck, and they'll kill him for us," Wynn mused with a pleased grin.

"No way," I shook my head and turned for the stairs. "I want to be up close and personal with Morpheus. No one fucks with my family and gets away with it."

The guys stared at me for a moment and then collectively laughed.

I pivoted, and my brows shot up to my hairline at their laughter. "What? What's so funny?"

"Nothing, love." Wynn followed after me. "You are just sounding more like a Durand every day."

"And that's a bad thing?" I asked, walking backward to the stairs.

"No," Wynn chuckled. "Not at all."

We marched up the stairs in one line, one united front against our enemies. One family.

At the top of the stairs, we split up. Drake headed to the kitchen, no doubt smelling the pie Gretchen had finished making. I wasn't holding my breath that he would save me any—damn pig.

The sun hadn't gone down yet, but thankfully, the tempered glass the Durands had put in recently made it easier for them to move around their own home without going up into flames. It was nice to have more light throughout the house, but the sun did limit the actions we could make to implement our plans.

"How long until sundown?" I asked over my shoulder as I walked through the dining room. I needed weapons, lots of weapons.

"Two hours, at least." Allister glanced at his phone before stopping at the bottom of the steps.

Wynn raced up the stairs, no doubt to get Antoine up to date. Rayne followed after him, but he didn't offer up his plan of action.

Making my way up behing them, I only made it a few steps up when Allister called out to me, "Hey, Piper?" He grabbed my wrist before I got too far up the stairs.

I twisted back around, climbing down the stairs until we were at eye level. "Yeah?"

"Thank you."

I frowned and cocked my head to the side. "For what?"

"For forgiving me. For loving me." He sighed and stared off at nothing. "For giving us all a reason to want to have eternity."

A small smile crept up my face, and I leaned into him. Cupping his face with my hands, I pressed my mouth to his. I kissed him deeply, as deeply as I felt for him and the others. I kissed him with everything that I had in me and then some. I pulled back, my breathing hard as I said, "I was floating through life before I walked into this house. It should be me that is thanking you."

Allister opened his mouth to say something else, but Jack appeared at the top of the stairs. The hand on my wrist tightened slightly, and I patted Allister's hand to calm him.

"Hey, Jack. How's it going?" I forced a smile, hoping it didn't show how much I wanted him to be gone.

Jack returned my smile with a more genuine one. However, I'd worked with the man long enough to know what the tightness around his eyes meant.

I sighed. "That bad, huh?"

This made Jack laugh. "I can't get anything by you." He dragged a hand through his dark hair and walked down the stairs to meet me. "Whoever is sabotaging you all is good near perfect. I'm going to have to call in a favor just to get a trace on the money. Then I can't even begin to explain the headache it's going to take to draw all the paperwork up to put an embargo in on the other company trying to buy the other businesses."

"Sounds like fun." I grimaced.

"This is the kind of thing I live for," Jack chuckled, stepping down another step closer to me. "I don't get this kind of action in Seabrick. It's all real estate closures and divorces. The real corporate cutthroat stuff is in the big cities."

"Why don't you move then?" Allister said with a hint of violence in his voice.

Jack met Allister's gaze as if he was just now seeing him. "I like small-town living. You know everyone and their dirty little secrets." When Allister and I tensed, Jack threw his head back and laughed. "I'm just kidding. I've never been one for intrigue unless it's on television. I wouldn't want a knife in my back."

"Or a pair of fangs," Allister whispered so low that Jack couldn't hear it.

I shot Allister a look before turning my attention back to Jack. "I know what you mean. Well, I'll let you get back to work. I have my own to do as well."

Jack inclined his head and moved to pass me on the steps. I waited until he was at the bottom of the steps before giving Allister one final look and then making my way up the stairs. When I hit the top step, the doorbell rang.

"I'll get it," Jack answered, changing his trajectory from the dining room to the front door. The figure behind the door was unfamiliar to me. Was it the hunters? Had they come to kill our family?

"Allister," I called out to him, worried for his safety. Unfortunately, I only distracted him from the door and who stood behind it.

The door opened, and a cloaked figure darted in, shoving himself and Jack into the room and out of the sunlight. The hood fell back seconds before his fangs sank into Jack's neck. Bright green eyes flashed, and deep auburn hair falling over a face I had just spent half an hour fantasizing over how to kill in the most painful way possible.

"Morpheus," I hissed, wanting nothing more than to rip his head from his spine. I made my way down the stairs, my eyes locked on the intruder not because he was killing Jack, but because I wanted to hurt him myself.

"Piper!" Allister shouted, stalking the line of the doorway where a massive streak of sunlight blocked his path from getting to Jack. I ran down the stairs and shut the door, keeping a wide distance from Morpheus. No matter how much I wanted to kill Morpheus, I didn't have any weapons, and against someone as old as him, I was likely to die before I got a hit in otherwise.

The moment his path was cleared, Allister shot across the foyer and crashed into Morpheus. Jack dropped to the ground in a boneless heap, and I knew before I even got to his side that it was too late. Jack's neck was savaged, not just bitten to feed but to hurt. Morpheus had damn near bitten through his neck, leaving Jack's eyes wide open, his mouth agape as if in mid-scream. He hadn't had a chance to scream, though. It all happened too fast. I grew angry. Angry for all that Morpheus had done against my family. For what he had done to me the last time I was at his club. And finally, for what he had done to Jack. He had to be stopped. Dead. Not by the hunters' hands. By mine.

Allister struggled with Morpheus, rolling around on the ground of the living room. Drake came out of the kitchen, saw what was happening, and came to Allister's aid. Drake grabbed Morpheus by one arm and Allister the other, but he was too strong for them to pin him down long enough to stake the bastard.

I grabbed a wooden chair sitting against the wall and slammed it against the back of the couch, breaking off an arm . The end was splintered enough that I would be able to drive it through Morpheus's heart, and it would all be over.

As I stalked over to the vampire in question, Morpheus's eyes widened, moving from side to side with desperate need. "No, don't. Please."

"Why shouldn't I?" I growled, twisting the wooden piece in my hand. "Your club is attacked the same night that Allister is there. Then your bartender tells them that all those murder victims were his dates. Tell me? Doesn't that sound like a conspiracy to you?"

Morpheus shook his head from side to side. "It wasn't me. I didn't do it."

"Hurry up, Piper," Drake growled, fighting to keep his hold on him. "He's way older than us. We can't hold him long."

I grinned. "Oh, it will be my pleasure." I took a step forward, lifting the homemade stake in the air, prepping to give him the final blow.

"You can't kill me," Morpheus tried once more.

"I think you will find I can." I tensed to bring the stake down when he stopped me once more with two words.

"The council," Morpheus cried out, pulling at his arms and trying to break free. "It's the vampire council."

I frowned and looked at the twins.

Drake shook his head. "He's lying. The council wouldn't do this. Not so indirectly."

Morpheus swallowed. "Yes, they would. They tipped off the hunters to my club because I helped you find your sire."

My lips pressed together tightly, my brows bunching together. "What does that have to do with Allister?"

"Who do you think is trying to frame him," Morpheus grunted. "It wasn't my bartender. He's not a vampire, but he is capable of being bribed or compelled to point the finger in Allister's direction."

My jaw tightened as I stared Morpheus down. Did I believe him? Did I put all of our lives in the hands of the one vampire alive I wanted dead more than anything else? Did I have a choice?

I looked to Allister and then to Drake.

Drake shook his head. "No. No way. We can't let him go after all this. Don't listen to him, Piper. It's a trick."

"Allister?" I swallowed, trying to find some other way. "What do you think?"

He looked to his brother and then to Morpheus before finally landing back on me. "I...I don't know. But I can't hold him much longer."

"I...I..." I glanced from one brother to the other. Stuck in the middle of an impossible decision I did not want to make. I did the only thing I could do. The only thing that ensured that my family would not hurt anymore at Morpheus's hands.

I attacked.

CHAPTER 18
Antoine

"THAT'S RIGHT. EVERYTHING IN the account needs to be transferred to the offshore account," I said to the frantic accountant on the phone in my office.

"Of course, Mr. Durand. Right away." Larry Hedgers' heart beat so fast I could hear it through the telephone. He wasn't guilty, just worried he was about to lose his best client because someone was trying to sabotage my family's assets. "Once again, I'm sorry to hear about your financial issues. I will make sure your money is protected. Give me a few hours and I'll-"

"One," I cut him off with a sigh as I leaned back in my chair. "You have one hour, and I want to see my account empty. Do not disappoint me, Larry." I hung up before the man could plead his case for more time. I didn't care what strings he had to pull. I would not let whoever was out to get us take everything away. I would do whatever I must to keep us financially sound.

Someone coming after our assets was unheard of. I'd never known anyone to go after us in such a way. Everyone who ever had an issue with us always came at us head on. Usually ending in bloodshed and then death. This was a form of attack I had not been prepared for. It couldn't have come at a worse time either.

With Allister's life hanging in the balance, I didn't need the extra stress of this. I had called the club to see if I could get a hold of Morpheus to no end. No one picked up the line, and when I tried his place of residency, I ended up with the same result. I was at my wit's end and not sure where to turn. We had no proof it was Allister or wasn't. The times Allister had told us he had come home on the nights in question, there was no footage of him coming home. Not like he hid from the cameras but as if the footage had been put on replay. No one and nothing showed on those nights, except for Allister leaving.

So far, that left us with nothing but a bloody trail all leading back to Allister.

I adjusted the cuffs of my shirt and huffed a breath of frustration. Why couldn't we figure this out? Morpheus being in the wind only made matters worse since we couldn't find out if it was him that was setting Allister up. I didn't think Morpheus had enough connections to be the one messing with our finances, but I wouldn't put it past him either. I just didn't have enough answers to any of my questions, and it was leaving me utterly helpless.

I hated that.

"I assume the news isn't good?" Darren asked from his seat across from me at my desk.

My gaze shifted over to him, and I stroked my jaw. "Nothing good, that is for certain. Larry will make sure our money is secure, and that is all we can do at the moment. Until Mr. Biggs can hunt down the paper trail of who or what is trying to destroy us, we cannot do anything but bide our time."

"And what of Allister?" Darren shuffled the papers in front of him and then stacked them neatly on the desk. "What are we to do about that problem?"

I growled. "I do not know. I could appeal to the council, but that would only draw their attention in our direction. We do not want them poking their noses around here if we can help it."

Piper being my human servant, was one thing but having a human servant who was also a vampire hunter was unheard of. I had no doubt the council would kill first and ask questions later. If there was anyone to ask questions from left alive.

No, I couldn't get them involved. It was too dangerous. We would simply have to figure it out ourselves.

"Perhaps, we should speak to Vincent," Darren suggested, standing from his chair and rounding the desk. "He seems like a reasonable man. I wouldn't imagine he would want to lose his new toy after he just got her."

I smirked and grabbed Darren by the wrist, pulling him forward. "No," I pressed my lips to his pulse, which jumped beneath my mouth, "I wouldn't think so."

Darren's breathing became heavy as he said, "There has to be some explanation. They wouldn't kill him just because they could."

I lifted my gaze to him. "Wouldn't they? I would think they would use any excuse they could to get rid of us."

"I think-" Darren's words cut off as his gaze jerked to the door as the doorbell went off. Frowning, Darren took a step back, and I released him. "Who could that be?" He moved toward the door, but I called after him as a flood of panic from Piper filled me, followed by the distinct scent of blood.

"Stay here," I ordered him and raced out the door. I made it to the top of the stairs in time to see Piper leaning over the prone form of Jack Biggs. The blood had belonged to him. It seeped out of him and covered the floor in a spreading pool of deep crimson. I swallowed back the hunger that reared at the sight of so much blood as Piper's head lifted, her attention on a fight going on in the living room.

Before I could begin my descent down the stairs, Piper was up off the floor and disappeared into the living room. Allister's voice called out, and he grunted in pain. A familiar voice I couldn't quite place responded in kind, and then Piper was talking to him.

Morpheus.

I saw blinding red and almost rushed into the room to rip the head off the traitorous bastard when the words coming out of his mouth stopped me. "The council! It's the vampire council."

“He's lying.," Draconius answered, coming from somewhere else. "The council wouldn't do this. Not so indirectly.”

“Yes, they would. They tipped off the hunters to my club because I helped you find your sire.” Morpheus would say anything to save his own skin but was this truth or a lie?

Piper seemed about as confused as I was when she asked, “What does that have to do with Allister?” That's my girl. Find out what he knows.

“Who do you think is trying to frame him,” Morpheus grunted. “It wasn't my bartender. He's not a vampire, but he is capable of being bribed or compelled to point the finger in Allister's direction.”

I moved further down the stairs but didn't enter the room, staying in the shadows of the doorway. If Piper could keep him talking before he saw me, then we might be able to find out what the hell was going on.

"No. No way," Draconius protested and grunted, "We can't let him go after all this. Don't listen to him, Piper. It's a trick."

"Allister?" Piper hesitated, her voice unsure of herself now. "What do you think?"

Unfortunately, Allister didn't know any more than the rest of us did. "I...I don't know. But I can't hold him much longer."

Since they weren't going to get anything else from him, I adjusted my jacket and stepped into the living room. Piper's hand came down to pierce the rotten manipulating vampire's heart, which I would have been more than happy to allow her to do if we didn't need him. I closed the distance between us and grasped her wrist, stopping her just before she pierced his chest.

"Antoine?" she gasped, staring up at me. "What are you doing? Morpheus needs to die."

I inclined my head, glaring at the vampire in question. "Agreed. However, now is not the time to take out our grievances. We need him alive." I met Morpheus's green relieved gaze. "If the council is indeed behind these inconveniences, then we need Morpheus."

"You believe him?" Piper snapped, jerking her arm from my grasp. "He's probably set this all up for some twisted game he will beat off to later."

Draconius snort laughed.

Morpheus glowered at Piper. "I hardly need to meddle in your lives to find my pleasure. I have many other enterprises that could easily satisfy my needs."

Piper snorted. "What? Eating babies?"

"Piper," I warned, though I was a bit proud of her smart mouth. Morpheus surely needed to be brought down a peg or two. "Now, Morpheus, why don't you enlighten us to this plot against us?"

Morpheus pulled on his arms. "I'm not speaking any further until you call your hounds off."

I glanced between the two brothers. We couldn't keep him standing here all day. The twins were strong, but not that strong. Not unless Marcus makes an appearance.

Then as if hearing my thoughts, Marcus came in from the dining room. His expression was questioning, and yet he held off. One of the best aspects of Marcus was his ability to compartmentalize. Marcus knew he would get his answers in due time and could focus on the problem at hand. Once Marcus took up a position near the twins, I gave them the go ahead to release him.

"Finally," Morpheus huffed, rubbing his arm and glaring at the twins. "I was two seconds away from ripping both of your boy toy's heads off."

Piper growled and lifted the hand holding the makeshift stake. "Try me, Morpheus. Just give me one reason."

"Love," Wynn said from behind us. I twisted slightly to see him leaning against the doorway. His lips were curved up in a pleased smile. "Don't do something you will regret."

"I won't regret it," Piper told him, scowling at the vampire in front of us. "I'll regret that I didn't make it last longer." She gestured to the lawyer's quickly cooling body in the foyer. "Just look what he did to Jack! I know the guy is a pain, but he didn't deserve that." Piper gestured the stake aggressively toward the man's body.

"Not that I'm upset that you have killed the man, though, it does put us back a bit in the paper trail," I sighed and shifted to stare at the dead man staining my foyer floor, before turning my attention back to Morpheus. "Why did you attack him?"

Morpheus had the decency to look embarrassed. "I haven't eaten all day, and the trip from the car to the door took a lot out of me. I haven't had to be underneath the full strength of the sun in a long time, I'm sad to say it drained me to the point of starvation, and I didn't think you would be happy if I bled your human servant." He looked pointedly at Piper, who tightened her grip on the stake and tensed.

"I'll show you who's going to be bleeding," she hissed as I put my arm out, stopping her from coming at him. "You can't keep protecting him. He doesn't deserve it."

"You've got that right." Rayne walked into the room, his brows drawn down. He had his silver container of blood in his hand and a straw sticking out of the top. "Unfortunately, as much as I want to tell you he's lying...I'm sad to say he's not." He sucked through the straw, making an annoying gurgling sound as he finished off the blood.

"You're kidding." Piper glanced at Rayne and then back to Morpheus. "You're telling me that this waste of space asshole is actually telling the truth?"

Rayne shrugged. "Sad but true. He does believe the council is behind all this."

"That's what I've been trying to tell you." Morpheus stalked over to Rayne and pulled the container from his hand. He tipped the container up and sucked down the last dribbles of blood, going so far as to lick along the insides of it. Morpheus shoved the container back at Rayne without so much of a thank you. "I have been running for my life since you called me about the hunters standing right outside my door."

"So, how do you know it's the council?" Rayne stared down into his cup, his mouth curled up in disgust. "What do you mean they contacted you?"

Morpheus glowered at Rayne. "Has anyone told you that is rather annoying?"

"Yes," everyone in the room announced at once, making Rayne flush red.

"Fuck all of you." Rayne stalked back into the other room.

"I still don't understand what we need him for?" Piper asked her anxiety and need to fight tittering in my chest. This wasn't going to end well.

"Piper," I placed a hand on her shoulder. "Why don't you take a moment? Let me speak with Morpheus and find out what he knows."

Piper's angry gaze shifted from Morpheus to me. "You want me to leave?"

I stepped closer to her, lowering my head down to her level. "The blood lust in your face is nothing like the emotions I am getting from you right now." Piper's eyes widened, and she ducked her head as if to hide. "Are you not moment's away from defying my orders?"

She wouldn't meet my gaze, her fingers tightening around the stake in her hands.

"Give it to me." I held my hand out.

Piper pulled her lower lip between her teeth, and her lids flipped up to show me the depths of her hate for the vampire before us. "No."

"Do not make me take it from you," I warned her, my own hand wrapping around the one holding the stake. Piper's eyes locked with mine for a moment longer, and for a second, I thought she might fight me on it before she nodded slightly, her hand releasing the stake into mine. "Thank you."

She didn't respond and simply stalked out of the room. Marcus followed after her without a word, as did Allister.

"Where are you going?" His twin called after him. "Don't you want to know why the council framed you?"

Allister shook his head. "No. I know I'm innocent and if they want to hurt us, take us down, they'll do it without me knowing all the details. Just figure out what we're going to do about it before we lose everything."

Draconius turned his gaze back to me and shrugged.

Sliding one hand into my pocket, I gestured with the other hand toward the couches. "Shall we? You might as well get comfortable. This may take a while."

CHAPTER 19
Piper

I STOMPED UP THE stairs making sure to make every step as loud as possible. Yes, I was being childish, but I really just wanted the pleasure of shoving my stake through his still undead heart.

Stopping in the hallway, I leaned against the wall, my body shaking. I could still feel his fangs in my neck. The way he ripped into my skin, his arms wrapped tightly around me. I knew he liked it. I could feel his hard on against my stomach as he bit into me. As he sucked my blood and caused me as much pain as possible.

"Piper," Marcus appeared in the hallway, kneeling beside me where I had sunk down on the ground without realizing it. "What's wrong?"

I sniffed and swiped at my face, the wetness catching me off guard. "I can still feel him." I grabbed at my neck, my fingers finding the place where he had bitten me - savaged me. There wasn't a scar, the vampire blood I had drunk had taken care of that, but that didn't mean I wasn't scarred on the inside. It was almost worse than Valentine's attack.

Almost.

With Valentine, there was the fear that no one would come to my rescue, that I really could die. It was worse and better with Morpheus. Yes, it caused the same kind of trauma Valentine had, but the guys had been there, making sure he wouldn't go too far. But having them there had made it all the worse. Like I blamed them for letting him hurt me even though I had been the one to volunteer to go in Rayne's place.

"Oh, Piper." Allister stood on my other side, his face pain-stricken. "I'm sorry Morpheus's presence has brought up such painful memories. I wished there was something I could do to take away your pain."

I looked up at Allister and then Marcus, my voice small and weak. I hated it. "Make me forget. Make it go away. Please."

Marcus gave Allister a questioning look.

Allister simply shrugged and knelt beside me. "Put your arms around my neck, I'm going to pick you up." He slid his arms beneath my back and legs, and I did as he asked. I pressed my face to the curve of his neck, inhaling his scent, and sighed.

I didn't care where he was carrying me to as long as it was as far away from Morpheus as possible. Marcus brought up the rear, and a tingling feeling swept through me. I was going to see Marcus naked. Marcus was going to see me naked. Suddenly, Morpheus didn't matter at all, and all I could feel was the anticipation in my stomach to get to a bedroom.

"Why here?" Marcus asked as we stepped into Allister's room.

Allister shrugged. "I don't know. Seemed like a good idea. Besides, my bed is bigger." He strode across the room and laid me down in the middle of the silk sheets. "Is this okay?" He asked me.

I glanced from him to Marcus, who stood at the end of the bed, unsure of himself. "Yeah. Yeah. This is okay."

"Good. Now take your clothes off." Allister grinned and climbed onto the bed next to me.

I laughed and shook my head. "Sometimes you and your brother are too much alike." The look on his face, the sudden dejection reminded me of what he had told me in the car, and I quickly backtracked. "I mean, you're not alike. Not at all. You're completely different. So different. You're not even twins to me. What doctor decided that? He was such a quack!" I rambled until Allister wrapped an arm around my waist and dragged me over to him, making me gasp.

"It's alright, Piper." He pressed his lips to my forehead and murmured softly, "I know I have issues, and they are things I will just have to work through, but you don't have to stop being you because of it."

I sank into his arms and smiled. "Good. Because I don't know how to be any other way."

Allister peered down at me, his expression full of so much light and love, it made me forget what we were doing here in the bedroom to begin with. Then he lowered his mouth to mine. Our lips brushed against one another in barely a whisper of a kiss as Allister's hands slid underneath the bottom of my shirt. His fingers trailed up my skin until he pushed the shirt all the way up to my armpits. I lifted my arms so he could remove it further, leaving me in just my bra.

For a moment, I became shy, my eyes skittering over to where Marcus sat on the edge of the bed. His gaze moved over my face like a hungry wolf, dying to take a bite out of me. I licked my lips and flushed under the heat of his stare. It was enough to make the big quiet man grin just like the wolf he portrayed.

Allister's lips pressed against my neck, his fingers going to the back of my bra. He had it unhooked in a matter of seconds. He pulled the straps down slowly over my shoulders and down my arms until only the cups were covering my chest. Shifting in his seat, he pulled me into his lap, so I faced Marcus before completely removing the last article of clothing, hiding me from Marcus's gaze.

"Your pants," Marcus said, his voice a low growl. "Let me help you."

I froze on the bed as he moved in closer, the hesitancy no longer there in his movements. Each touch of his hand on my skin on the waistband of my pants was that of a confident man who knew what he wanted, and he wanted it now.

When he had them undone, I had to lay back against Allister so I could raise my hips. Marcus drew the pants down my legs, my lacy thong the only thing covering that last bit of me. Without even touching me there, my center was already hot and wet. It pulsated with the need to be touched and praised.

"You smell so good," Allister growled into my ear, his hands roaming over my stomach and coming up to cup my breasts. "No woman's scent has ever driven me as wild as yours. Don't you think, Marcus?"

The larger man knelt between my thighs, his dark orbs eating up every inch of my flesh. It was so intense, part of me was afraid to let him touch me while the other half screamed for relief.

I chewed on my lip while Marcus wrapped his hand around my ankle, my shoes having been discarded with my pants. He pressed his mouth to the arch of my foot, then along my heel and up my calf. He paid particular attention to the back of my knees, something I had just recently found to be an erotic place for me. I clung to Allister's biceps, my eyes closing as I embraced the sensations taking over me.

"Eyes open, Piper." Allister murmured, flicking my nipples. "You wanted us to make you forget, then you need to burn this picture into your mind."

I didn't need to see them to remember this image. Allister behind me and Marcus between my legs? I'd already dreamed of this scenario, and yet it was nowhere close to as good as the real thing.

Marcus's mouth finally reached the inside of my thigh, and my hips arched up, searching for the friction I needed to find my release. To my dismay, Marcus bypassed my panty-clad core. He moved to the other thigh, working his way down the leg as he'd done the other one, except now it was less thrilling and more frustrating.

"Patience," Marcus whispered against my skin, his gaze sliding up to mine. "In good time. I promise."

I whimpered as his mouth found the back of my knee once more, and my nails bit into Allister's arms. "Please. No more. No more."

Allister hissed but didn't complain. To Marcus, he said, though, "You might want to hurry it up. She's gotten a lot stronger since she started training every day."

Smiling up at Allister, I asked, "Are you afraid I can take you down?"

Those memorizing spirals of blue and green eyes peered down at me, and the grin he gave me had my breath catching. "You've already taken me down, Piper. With your smile. Your laughter. With your smart mouth and soft body. You've destroyed all of us, and we'd happily do it again just to have a moment with you."

"God, you're going to make me cry." I sniffed and smiled a watery smile.

"We can't have that," Allister chuckled. "No tears in the bedroom." He kissed the side of my neck loudly and slobbery making me laugh.

Suddenly a hot wet mouth covered the front of my panties, and I almost jumped out of my skin as Marcus sucked on my clit through the material. "Fuck," I hissed, trying to move my hand down to Marcus, but Allister kept me locked into place.

"I think someone felt a bit left out," Allister mused in my ear, his hands lifting my arms up and around his neck. "Hold on to me and just let go. It's been said Marcus is the best of us all at this."

I tried to make some coherent smart-ass response, but all I could get out was an "Uh-huh?"

Marcus's large hands held my thighs, lifting my hips just enough, so he had the leverage he needed. He hadn't even removed my panties, and already I was on the verge of coming apart.

"I... I can't..." I breathed my chest rising and falling quickly. "I need to...I'm going to..."

"That's it, Piper." Allister purred in my ear, his silvery tongue working its magic. "Just let go."

My head fell back, and my body spasmed as it fought against the building down low. It was then that Marcus drew the material of my thong to the side and pressed his full mouth against me. I couldn't hold it back any longer. I screamed my release, my nails driving into the back of Allister's neck, and the scent of blood filled the air.

Allister didn't try to get me to stop, his hands moving up and down my arms, murmuring dirty things in my ears as I came down.

It was as if I had melted into a puddle on the bed. My limbs didn't work, and my eyes were heavy. I couldn't imagine getting up any time soon.

"Oh, baby," Allister tapped the side of my face. "He isn't even close to being finished."

I forced my eyes open to peer down at the vampire between my legs. He straightened and wiped a hand over his chin before licking the remnants of me off his mouth. Eyes locked with mine, Marcus grabbed the sides of my thong and slowly inched them down my legs.

Giving myself a moment to recuperate, I exclaimed, "Finally! One of you doesn't rip my clothes off my body. You have no idea how expensive my clothes budget has become."

Marcus smirked, before balling up my thong and bringing it to his nose. My whole body flushed as I watched him inhale my scent. It shouldn't have been more intimate than the fact that he had just had his mouth on me, but somehow it was. Watching him made my skin tight and itchy.

Soon the feeling was pushed aside for the predatory look in Marcus's eyes as he tucked my thong into his pants pocket. "For later," he told me before finding his place between me once more.

An hour later and I certainly wasn't thinking about Valentine or Morpheus. Hell, I could barely breathe, let alone move, but there were things still to be done, and I wanted to make sure the two men still fully clothed in bed with me were going to be safe.

"We should head downstairs," I prompted, playing with the strands of Allister's hair. "They're probably done, don't you think?"

Allister shrugged a shoulder. "Maybe. But do you think you can walk?"

I wiggled between the two of them, Allister at my back and Marcus's head on my hip. "Well, maybe if I lost a few hundred pounds, I might be able to manage it."

Chuckling, the two of them shifted so I could slide out of bed. Immediately, my legs tried to go out from underneath me. I grabbed the bedpost to hold myself up and giggled. "I guess you weren't kidding about being the best at that, huh?"

Marcus simply smiled at me.

Slowly this time, I searched the ground for my clothes, pulling on my bra and then my shirt before finally finding my pants. I paused and turned to Marcus. "I'm not getting my underwear back, am I?"

"No," Marcus's low rumbling voice sent another wave of pleasure through me.

I shook it off and grabbed my pants, deciding to just go without. "Fine. Keep them. I have others."

Marcus made an amused sound as if they too might end up in his belongings eventually. At this rate, it was damn well likely.

"Okay," I breathed, "I'm dressed. Let's go."

The two of them followed me off the bed and to the door. My legs felt a bit like a calf learning to walk, but I was determined to have a clear mind, so maybe I could revisit this again tonight. If Marcus was that good at this, then he had to be even better at the rest of it, right?

Smiling to myself, I slipped my hand into Allister's and then into Marcus's. They both looked at me surprised, but didn't pull away. We walked down the hallway hand in hand toward the stairs. We could still hear the voices of those we had left behind in the living room, and the way Antoine was sounding, it wasn't going well.

"Think we should go break it up?" I peered at the two of them, not waiting for their answer as I released their hands to walk down the stairs. Each step caused my pants to rub against my sensitive clit, and I grabbed the banister for dear life.

Allister chuckled behind me, earning him a glare.

"It's not funny."

"Piper? Are you calm now?" Antoine called out to me from the living room.

Sighing, I finished walking the rest of the way down the stairs to answer. Before I had a chance to respond, the doorbell rang for the second time in one day. We were becoming the place to be. Shifting slightly, my legs a bit wobbly, my eyes went to Marcus as a zing of pleasure reminded me of what we had just done.

"Do you really want to answer that?" Allister leaned against the banister. "I mean, it went so well the first time." He jerked his head toward the stain on the floor where Jack's body had once been.

"Oh, come on." I smiled back at him. "Things can't get any worse."

"Great." Drake snorted. "You just had to say that. Of course, things are going to get worse now."

I rolled my eyes. "Hey, I could still kill Morpheus." I grinned at the club owner. "That would make everything today better."

"Piper," Antoine warned though his lips ticked up at the sides. "We aren't killing anyone today."

Scoffing, I reached for the door handle. "Don't say that until we know who is on our doorstep."

"True," Rayne agreed with a grin.

My grin spread wider as I turned to the open door. I sagged and frowned at who stood before me. "Damn, Drake. You were right."

"Hello, Piper." Vincent, the president and leader of the vampire hunters smiled at me arrogantly from in front of a black limo. His black curls shined with too much product as his dark eyes lit up with amusement. "I believe you wished to speak to me. Something about a vampire council?"

I frowned and stepped toward the limo cautiously. "How did you know about that?"

"I bugged your home, of course." His grin broadened as his gaze shifted over my shoulder. "Please do not fret for your vampire lover's safety. I have explained to Mizuki it was all a misunderstanding, he will be safe from harm."

I crossed my arms over my chest and stopped before him. "What's the catch?"

"Why must there be a catch, my dear?" His grin was almost as bright as the light shining off the two diamond studs in his ears. Too bad, I wasn't buying it.

"There's always a catch with you. What do you want in return?"

"Piper be careful," Rayne called out behind me. "He is trying very hard to keep his mind blank right now."

I waved him off and narrowed my eyes on Vincent. "So? What is it?"

Vincent held the limo door open for me with a gentlemanly bow. "Let us take this conversation elsewhere, and I would be happy to ease all your fears."

The ball of tension behind me was palpable. The guys were not going to let me go anywhere with him on my own. I didn't particularly want to go with him either. Unfortunately, I didn't know what other choices I had.

"And where would we go?" I inquired, cocking my head to the side. "What can't you say to me here where I am protected? Why do we need to be alone?"

"I have offered you no violence. It hurts that you would think so little of me." Vincent placed a hand on his chest, his face the epitome of distress. When his words didn't sway me, Vincent straightened, clearing his throat. "Very well, I can admit that I do not trust the council has not also bugged your home with their own listening devices. I wish our discussion not to be overheard."

"And you don't think they haven't done your limo and the headquarters as well?" I pointed out with a shake of my head. "You aren't untouchable."

"That I am aware of," Vincent adjusted his garish suit jacket and grew serious. "I do not make this offer often. However, you have somehow gained the attention of the vampire council, a group I have longed to see put to heel. Which means that I need you if I am to ever get any of my hunters within breathing distance of them."

I pursed my lips and lifted my chin. "What exactly are you offering?"

Vincent cleared his throat and shifted in place. "Your freedom and no future attacks on your family...in exchange for helping us take down the council."

The others gasped behind me, no doubt feeling precisely what I was feeling. Relief. Excitement. Uncertainty. Fear.

"And if we can't?" I pushed, needing to know the full scope of this offer.

Vincent shrugged a shoulder, tapping his fingertips of each hand in a steeple. "Then, things go back to the way they were before. You helping my hunters find vampires and taking them out. Perhaps in another decade, we might come to some other arrangement?"

He had me, and he knew it. Damn it.

I glanced back at the others who had the same mistrusting but hopeful expression on their faces. My eyes drifted over to Antoine, searching his face for some kind of message. Did he approve of this deal, or was I rash to think it too good to be true?

When my eyes locked with his, Antoine wasn't looking at me. He was looking at Morpheus. The vampire was sweating buckets, and I didn't even know vampires could sweat like that. Something about my making a deal with Vincent made Morpheus nervous. It only made my decision easier.

Turning back to Vincent, I held my hand out to him. "You have a deal."

Vincent wrapped his warm, surprisingly soft hand around mine and shook it. "Good. Then shall we?" He gestured to the limo, waiting for me to enter the open door.

Taking one more look at the guys, I tried to reassure them with my eyes that everything was going to be okay. That I was going to be fine. We would all get out of this alive, and with any luck, I'd be freed from my debt to the vampire hunters.

Yeah. One could dream.

ABOUT THE AUTHOR

Erin Bedford is an otaku, recovering coffee addict, and Legend of Zelda fanatic. Her brain is so full of stories that need to be told that she must get them out or explode into a million screaming chibis. Obsessed with fairy tales and bad boys, she hasn't found a story she can't twist to match her deviant mind full of innuendos, snarky humor, and dream guys.

On the outside, she's a work from home mom and bookbinger. One the inside, she's a thirteen-year-old boy screaming to get out and tell you the pervy joke they found online. As an ex-computer programmer, she dreams of one day combining her love for writing and college credits to make the ultimate video game!

Until then, when she's not writing, Erin is devouring as many books as possible on her quest to have the biggest book gut of all time. She's written over thirty books, ranging from paranormal romance, urban fantasy, and even scifi romance.

Come chat me up!
www.erinbedford.com
Facebook.com/erinrbedford
twitter.com/erin_bedford
Don't forget to follow me on Goodreads, Pinterest, Instagram, and YouTube!

www.ingramcontent.com/pod-product-compliance
Lightning Source LLC
Chambersburg PA
CBHW070928190726
48292CB00004B/1153